SMALL BEAUTY

SMALL BEAUTY

JIA QING WILSON-YANG

METONYMY PRESS

Montreal, QC

This is a work of fiction. Names, characters, events, and incidents are either the products of the author's imagination or used in a fictitious manner. Any resemblance to actual persons, living or dead, or actual events is purely coincidental.

Metonymy Press
Montreal, QC
metonymypress.com

Printed in Quebec by Le Caïus du livre
Cover design by LOKI
Second Printing - September 2016

Library and Archives Canada Cataloguing in Publication

Wilson-Yang, Jia Qing, author
      Small beauty / Jia Qing Wilson-Yang.

Includes some text in Pinyin.
ISBN 978-0-9940471-2-0 (paperback)

      I. Title.

PS8645.I49S63 2016   C813'.6   C2016-902886-0

Deepest thanks to Ashley and Oliver for all their work editing and for holding space for this book, to Gordon Shean for his careful consideration of the story and for suggesting the plant, to Alvis Choi for checking the Pinyin, to Morgan Page and Heidi Cho for reading an early version and offering much-needed feedback, to Violet King for love, guidance, and laughter, to my family for generous support, and to my ancestors for checking in on me and offering encouragement.

With love and gratitude to all my elders,
present and departed

She is sitting at the back of a canoe. Floating in the middle of the bay. She is far enough from shore that she can no longer see the glow of the lights in the nearby town, just a false halo outlining the trees to the south. Her gaze moves from the light and out to the lake. Into the true night, where she sees the water still enough to mirror the stars and moon, erasing the horizon and giving her the feeling she has paddled an hour from shore to achieve. She is isolated and contained in this. She imagines herself suspended in the centre of a perfect sphere, memories swirling around her like smoke or winter breath.

UNSOLICITED GUIDANCE

THE WEATHER HAS softened. With slower winds, the trees look suddenly taller. Snow melts off their branches. They are hatching.

Even with the calming wind, Sandy's old parka and her double scarves aren't enough. She is freezing. Winter and snow are things she loves. She used to think she loved the cold, but now she understands she had just romanticized it, melted the memories, as if walking in someone else's dream.

The city, despite all the ways it pushed callouses into her, softened her tolerance for cold. She used to spend whole days in snowy woods, lost and a little stoned. Now she stays on the path as best as she can, for a few hours at most. She feels her blood heating up as she takes step after careful step, keeping a pace that is more habit than intention. Her feet break through the crust of frozen snow, lost for an instant below the brittle curvature of the trail. A shell cracking. Her thighs sting from the cold, and her sweat freezes on the hair of her brow. Where she had been engulfed in the landscape as a child, she is now caught in her body's reaction to it.

As she walks up to the house, a flock of birds scatter from a tree out back and seem to hover around the house a moment. They are held in a fragmented union before setting off in all directions. Snow grinds beneath her feet, packed down into the driveway from her walking to and from the road. The sound welcomes her from the concession onto the property. She passes fences, fallen and no longer dividing road from field. She has been walking around the woodlot across from the house, ambling through the trails with Hazel, Sandy's dog.

It was the phone that scattered the birds. "I have to figure out how to turn down the ringer," she says under her breath, cloudy and visible. Trying to run in Sandy's snow boots only makes her feel as though she is faster, but it does little more than heat her up. The answering machine uses some kind of mini tape that she hasn't been able to find anywhere in the house.

"Hello?" She grabs the phone off the living room wall. She is out of breath. Boots on, tracked-in snow melting a path behind her. Hazel approaches, tail wagging, pushing her wet nose into the back of Mei's hand.

"Hello, darling! Jesus, Mei, you took your time getting to the phone. It must have rung thirty times— you're lucky I'm *busy* looking for a job. I just put you on speaker and waited for your answering machine to pick up. Which it didn't. You *do* get cell reception out there. I know you do, I looked it up. I don't see why I need to call you at this number and wait for ages while you do whatever it is you're doing—god, you're breathing heavy. Did I interrupt you? Is there someone special there? Is there? I told you! You'll go to the woods and meet one of those *woodsy* dykes! And she'll—"

"Hi Annette," Mei interrupts. Her lungs are taking in the warmer air of the house, softening. "There are no woodsy dykes in my house. I wish. Just me. And Hazel."

"Who is *Hazel?*"

"Sandy's dog. I think she's a cattle dog. Or maybe a weird Corgi mix? Do they have Corgis on farms?" Mei unzips Sandy's parka and walks into the kitchen, boots clunking on the linoleum.

"Right. The dog. I forgot. I don't know about Corgi dogs or whatever. Why are you asking me? Aren't there people around that you can ask?" Mei can hear, beneath the sarcasm, her friend's worry.

"Well. Yeah. Probably." Mei plays with the phone cord and clumsily sits down at the kitchen table, pausing before kicking her boots off, an imprecise action that takes her socks off as well.

"You still haven't talked to anyone, have you?" The question is more of a statement; Annette knows her friend.

Almost ashamed, Mei pauses and says, "I, uh ... I have." She stands, silently wincing as she steps barefoot into a pool of melted snow.

"Liar. Two months! You've been gone two months. You're connecting with the dog? Don't make me come out there. Go make some friends. You grew up in the woods. Go make a fire and wear practical shoes."

She is right, Mei needs to get out. The demanding love of her pushy friend is cold water on a sleepy face.

"Sandy grew up here, not me. I just visited sometimes." Mei walks to the sink and stares out the window over the back of the property. The goose has returned and is looking in the window. She should probably stop feeding it.

Annette won't let Mei dodge the direction of the conversation. "For, like, months at a time..." Mei can hear Annette rolling her eyes.

"It's just that ... I just don't know how to meet people here." She knows Annette won't buy it, but she is in retreat, losing the conversation and firing off poorly aimed defences.

"That's bullshit. Is there a bar?"

Mei is caught. Sliding the small, mostly dead plant on the counter closer to her, she sticks her finger in the soil. Still damp.

"Yeah, there's a bar."

She had moved the plant from Bernadette's room to the window by the kitchen a few weeks ago to see if it needed more light. No change yet. The pile of brown crumpled heart-shaped leaves hasn't sprouted anything new.

"Well. It can't be *that* different out of the city. Go to a bar. Sit there. Talk to someone. Introduce yourself."

Mei can't be irresolute any longer. "Why did you call?" Mei crosses her arms, pinning the phone between her cheek and shoulder and leaning on one hip, picking dead leaves off the plant.

"Harsh, my love, harsh. I called because you wanted to know if anything happened with welfare. I called the automated system. They think you're still in the city, trying to look for work and not living in your dead cousin's empty house. In the winter. *Alone...*" She pauses. "Anyway, they want you to go to a resumé-writing workshop in two weeks."

"Agh. Those are *the worst*! Everyone hates being there, even the facilitators. People ask things like, 'I was a brain surgeon before I moved to Canada and now I can't even get a job cleaning hotels. What should I put on my resumé other than the fifteen university degrees and decades of experience I have?' And the facilitator will say something like, 'What font did you use?' It's racist. I bet I can skip it and they won't notice. I'm supposed to be inept at getting a job anyways, right? That's why I'm on welfare." Mei leans further back on her hip and supports herself in the doorway between the kitchen and the living room. The solidity of the house confirms her position.

"Whatever you say. If they cut you off, it wasn't because of me."

"I know, Annette, I know."

"I worry about you out there alone."

The friends continue talking, Annette catching Mei up. Her clients, her dates. Good ones and bad. Mei hears about what's happening with the women at the drop-in the two of them used to visit, and new dramas she is happy to miss out on. How Annette is sick of being the only Asian transsexual left in Dundurn, which they both know is a lie. Annette is one of the only people Mei wants to keep in contact with from the city, and the only one whose phone number seems to work.

Her friend Connie's number isn't working these days, a semi-regular occurrence. She probably just missed a few payments. Once Mei hangs up, she cradles the phone and resumes looking through the window in the kitchen. What if she stopped feeding the goose and it didn't leave? It seems like it will be around all winter. She looks down at Hazel, who is licking her pant leg.

Seeing a stale heel of bread on the counter, Mei asks the dog, "Who says I'm not making friends?" She walks to the fridge and pulls out a handful of spinach to put in a bowl. "Ya see? A snack for our *friend*," she says proudly, taking the bowl out to the goose.

ɔ

Aside from her interaction with the grocery store clerks every week or so, she doesn't meet anyone until the spring.

———·———

S HE IS SITTING in her apartment in Dundurn, look-ing out at the trees frantic in a storm. Hazel is leaning into her on the sofa. Still acclimatizing to not having Sandy around, they are both surprised at the comfort of someone who understands. Mei frequently finds herself speaking to Hazel, who listens attentive-ly, making calm and steady eye contact. Hazel in turn has started following Mei around the apartment and sleeping in her bed. Life is unfamiliar and sad without Sandy. There is no other way for it to happen.

The wind is tremendous. It is the night before she will leave the city. She closes the blinds, so only the sound of the storm is in the room. The windows shake and rain hits the glass as if the building has been top-pled over to receive the water pouring out of the sky.

ↄ

Mei has lived in Dundurn most of her life; its smells and sounds are familiar. Her mother, Jun, new-ly married and pregnant, moved from Herbertsville to Dundurn into the home of her husband, Mei's fa-ther. Mei doesn't remember much of the house; she had either blocked it out or was too young. Jun moved out when Mei was barely a toddler, taking her to live in South Dundurn, away from her father's house. Mei heard he had moved out of Dundurn, somewhere out east, maybe west. She has no clear recollection of who he is, just shadowy memories, moments on pause in her mind. Her thoughts slow when she reflects on her childhood, a fly in molasses.

A few years ago, she almost finished a year at the university and dropped out. Her mother, claiming this to be the last transgression she could handle, threatened to move back to China and leave Mei alone in the city, as she had threatened to do for years. Then Mei told her mother she was a transsexual, something Jun had long suspected but Mei had never openly confirmed, and her mother set plans in motion to leave Dundurn. They had been living together, and when her mother gave notice, Mei had to find another place to live. And Jun was gone, possibly back to China, where she had not lived since she was a small child.

After a frantic search, Mei found a place in the neighbourhood she'd lived in when she was born, her father's neighbourhood in the west end. Not the nice west end, but the not-so-nice west end beside it. Mei moved not to recapture a childhood she never had, but because rent was cheaper. She feels no nostalgia for her neighbourhood. The park is not a park she remembers visiting as a child; there is no tree she recalls climbing. One thing is certain: in this neighbourhood she will not cross paths with family or anyone who knew her when she was a boy. Even if her father were still living in Dundurn, she doubts she would remember his face enough to recognize him.

ↄ

The next morning she and Hazel are in the park. On their walk, the markings of the wind fill the street. Traffic lights are unlit and paper plates are scattered like wet leaves. Maple, oak, and poplar all seem to have grown coffee cups and thrown them to the ground in the violence of the storm, as though protesting the departure of a stubborn lover.

The level fields of the park let the wind run unhindered. Leaves caught up in the running give the illusion of a perpetually moving ground, a river of damp leaves and grass. Hazel approaches the field as though it were a lake, first with excitement and then, reaching the shallows of the moving leaves, she is startled. The energy swirls around her, moving every hair on her body. The total stimulation of an autumn reckoning.

Mei remembers the radio broadcast, the weekend science program. *Weather systems are always trying to balance. High pressure is trying to get to low, while low pressure is making space for high pressure zones. The energy of thunderstorms is a rebalancing of charges in the atmosphere. The rain moves in cycles. It is the sky too full of water to take on any more. Unless the temperature rises.* She imagines a huge river running through the sky above her, pulling the banks. Flooding the shore.

Then Hazel is off and back with a clump of feathers in her mouth, gathered at the quill by a piece of flesh. Mei looks around for the other parts of the bird, to predict the movement of the dog as she attempts to coax the feathers from Hazel's mouth. As Hazel reluctantly places the clump on the ground, Mei notices another part of the bird. Mixed in with the pieces of a shattered burl on a fallen branch, there is a single wing. It is separated perfectly from the body of the bird. No blood or tendons, no evidence that the wing was ever connected to anything. It has not been chewed on or torn apart by animals. The only thing in the city untouched by the storm.

Absorbing the perfect separation of a wing, the turmoil of the park, she imagines a heavenly order, an intervention. An absent authority has decided a purpose must be served. She cannot decide if it is cruel or ambivalent. Hazel walks over and picks up the wing in her mouth. She drops it immediately as though it is hot.

Dead leaves pour into the playground, flooding the slide. There is a car alarm. Or a motor, unoiled and squeaking regularly in the alley beside the park. They walk away from the wing, toward the sound, toward home. But the sound stops before they can determine its origin.

ↄ

When Mei heard that some folks were leaving the city for the weekend and driving through Herbertsville, she had asked them for a ride up to Sandy's house. Her house now. Since Sandy died, she has had trouble concentrating, trouble sleeping. Hazel needs to walk every day, which makes her go outside, but if it weren't for Annette being a generally pushy friend, Mei wouldn't have seen or spoken with anyone, really. At least in Herbertsville, Hazel will have a nicer place to walk around.

Waiting outside of her apartment with the dog, she takes a deep breath of the autumn air, brittle and metallic in her lungs. She has a backpack of clothes and a black cloth bag holding a notebook, something to read, and her wallet. The bag has the name of a grocery store peeling off of it. Annette connected her with Bina, the driver, who Mei has never met before. Annette couldn't come by to see Mei off. She was busy with some new client who wanted to spend a week with her at a downtown hotel. Mei got semi-regular texts letting her know about the client, but more often about the food Annette was eating.

Mei has not let herself acknowledge Sandy's death. The practical, factual results of it she understands. He is not around; she has his dog, his house, and his truck. She cannot call him to tell him how weird this all is. These are painful realities, but she has diminished the weight of them for herself and with others. Despite having known Annette for nearly a decade, she has only spoken to her of Sandy in passing. She has never spoken of him to Connie, a woman from the drop-in she visits a few times a month at her apartment across town.

Family is a tricky, shifting shoreline of a topic. Mei's personal life has been pried into by community workers, doctors, counsellors, curious strangers, and police, and she rarely brings up the topic with other trans women. With them she finds the space to talk about other things that matter, like favourite foods, sex, or art. She could do that with Sandy, she recalls, exhaling a white cloud of warm air into the cold morning. Well, less about sex and more about radio shows, she amends her reflection. A car arrives, and the driver leans over a passenger and pushes uneven black hair out of her eyes. Mei recognizes the passenger but cannot remember his name. She has seen him at a trans-only drop-in downtown. The driver looks like someone Mei went to university with. She has a moment of panic, dreading having to explain who she is versus who she used to be. The driver's window rolls down.

"You Mei?"

Mei nods, smiling. Not her old classmate, no need for explanations.

"I'm Bina, this is Rick. I'll open the trunk." Then, noticing Hazel, "Cute dog."

Hazel's tail wags lightly as Mei exhales, relieved.

Ꙩ

In the car, Rick acknowledges too frequently his privileges, things Mei can tell without his naming of them. They seem to expand with every admission. She makes him nervous but tries to speak without judgement. Sandy had complained that she was too harsh too quickly with people, expecting everyone to have reached her conclusions when she had. He was unnecessarily abrasive with this criticism, but it held truth. The last time she had seen him, about a month before he died, she had been complaining about someone at the drop-in who had been giving her a hard time. Sandy couldn't understand why Mei wouldn't just confront them directly and have it done with. Mei didn't think it was appropriate. Sandy asked if Mei had complained to anyone else about them, people who knew them. Mei didn't answer. Sandy told her, "You're a jerk, gossiping about things you don't have the guts to say. Where the fuck did you learn that? Slapping them in the face would be nicer. At least they could defend themselves." It had actually been a great visit, they'd made dumplings, watched a movie, fun things.

She notices she is absently listening to Rick, repeating herself, offering only "Yeah, totally" and "For sure" to the conversation, like a lacklustre surfer. Absently passing her hand through Hazel's fur, she decides this is not the time or place to work on confronting people. Picking up on the fact that Mei is no longer focussing on the conversation, Rick trails off. Mei, sensing she may have hurt him, lets out a last "Definitely" with as much sincerity as she can muster, but it does little to help. They listen to the radio. *Leave it all behind. Forget your life before. Make up your mind, live for now!* The previous song had the same message: risk everything, do something adventurous, follow a devastatingly handsome young white boy to sure and certain heartbreak. Cut the strings that hold you.

"Do you folks ever think that there's, like, a place where all these people who ran off together in these songs end up and how they're all cynical now, having realized they risked everything for a foolishly timed jump, based on a crush that wasn't going anywhere? I would watch that reality show," Mei wonders, too earnestly, before realizing Rick and Bina are doing just that. She feels heat rise to her cheeks. The two laugh awkwardly while Rick scans the CDs clipped to the sun visor.

"That's really sad about your uncle," Bina offers.

"He was my cousin, but thanks..."

౨

Before Bernadette died, when Mei was coming into her true self as a teenager, she would visit Sandy and Bernadette. Sandy would drive down to the city, pick her up at her mother's house, and take her up for the weekend, or sometimes a week or two at a time. She had always been close with Sandy, and when Jun started to pick up on what kind of person Mei was going to be, Sandy was there for her, not really understanding, but ready to take her someplace she could be herself. Up in Herbertsville, Mei could wear what she wanted; she could let herself be a girl, not the cagey teenage boy she loathed to be in the city. Bernadette seemed to love the visits, using Mei's chosen name and, most importantly, not reporting everything back to Jun. In the end Jun found out about Mei and what she had been doing on her visits to the country. Jun had berated Bernadette for "ruining" Mei, and had said many other things in Mandarin that Mei couldn't understand. Now, driving through Herbertsville—past the stores, out onto the concession—Mei feels like she is coming home.

ɔ

When they arrive at the house it is late afternoon. The sky is welcoming, open to large white clouds, steely in the autumn air. Thanking Bina for the ride, she walks up the drive to the door. Hazel runs around the property and chases a white cat across the porch and off into the fields behind. The house is small, set back from the road. The concrete foundation, visible below light blue vinyl siding, is starting to crack. It is solitary, surrounded by fields owned and farmed by someone else. The lawyer had given Mei a brown envelope, so unremarkable it had to be official. In it, she found a copy of Sandy's bank information, his drivers insurance, and four keys. One for the truck in the driveway and three for the house—all the same key. Counting them in her hand, she runs her finger over them. One for Sandy, one for his mother, and a spare, she guesses. The bitting of two of the keys is smooth from years of turning, the tidal motion of ingress and exit. The third is sharper. It has not been part of the daily motions of the household.

Pausing for a second before deciding she is being too sentimental, she opens the door and walks inside. Sandy had been living here alone since Bernadette passed away. Sandy often talked about getting an apartment in Dundurn, saying he needed a change. His work was between here and the city, and he wanted to be around fewer white people. But he never did. It was harder to leave than he let on.

The house is a bungalow. Two bedrooms, a living room, a bathroom, and a small kitchen. A basement, more of a cellar, is accessed through a trap door in the kitchen floor. It has a small folding staircase. The house is as she remembers it. Everything intentional. A small table by the door for keys and purses. A pad of paper perfectly centred on the kitchen table, a photo of Sandy squared to the corner of the fridge. Peering slowly at the bedrooms, she sees tightly made beds. Even the dishes in the cupboards are placed with purpose. Bernadette had kept the home immaculate when Mei was younger. It is dusty now, but everything is still arranged perfectly. Sandy grew up having to keep things in order.

Mei relaxes into a feeling of safety, knowing that she is in Herbertsville with a guide: Hazel is a local. Mei has only ever been a visitor here; even the years she spent as a child in the town with her mother were always understood to be temporary. Hazel had burst past Mei when she opened the door, tail wagging, expecting to see Sandy. The door opens into the living room, where an arm chair and a sofa face the front window. There is a doorway into the kitchen from the living room. In and out of each of the rooms Hazel searches for him, his scent enfolded in the house. As she paces, she lets out a small quick whine, confused at the empty house, unsettled. Mei's eyes swell. She hangs her head over the sink, wanting so much to cry. To sob. Her head aches from wanting such catharsis, but she cannot. Wetting her hands under the tap, she rubs cold water over her face and looks for Hazel. Mei walks out of the kitchen and down the narrow hall behind the living room. Off the hall are the two bedrooms and the bathroom. Each of the bedrooms has the same view, a few large old trees in a small yard that ends abruptly at the beginning of a tended field. She finds the dog is staring out the back window in Bernadette's room, wagging her tail and watching a small flock of geese in the backyard.

"I wish I could let go that easily. Jerk," Mei grumbles, stepping out of the hallway into Bernadette's room. Springs creak as Mei lets Bernadette's bed take her weight. The support allows exhaustion she is not expecting. Sandy and Bernadette had shared Bernadette's room when he was young, before Nai Nai

died. Mei remembers the small cot Sandy slept on
beside Bernadette's bed. Nai Nai's door was always
closed, but the smell of incense Jun brought back from
Dundurn would slip out, mixing with the air in the
kitchen.

On the dresser in Bernadette's room, away from
the window, there is a dead or dying plant. Dried heart-
shaped leaves contorted, their moisture pulled back
into the roots. It looks out of place in the house. It is
uniquely neglected. Mei decides to move it to the kitch-
en. Afterward, she enjoys the support of Bernadette's
single bed.

Night has set in when she wakes up, her
head below a window. Mei decides she will sleep in
Bernadette's room while she is here. She had thought
about staying in Sandy's room, but Bernadette's is
where Hazel seems to have chosen after pacing through
the house, searching. It has been five years since she
died. She survived her mother and she may as well
have survived her sister. Jun had not come home for
the funeral, and neither Mei nor Sandy had had any
way of contacting her. When Bernadette was close to
passing, she had said she was happy she wasn't going
to survive her son. She had no way of knowing how
close she came to doing so.

Mei is sleeping, but barely. She cannot settle.
The crickets seem to shatter the warm night. It is all
she can hear. Stirring, she feels weight on the mat-
tress—not the weight of Hazel. She sits up to see an

old woman sitting near the foot of the bed.

"Xiao Mei, good you came here. This a good place to remember who you are."

Mei's eyes are heavy with sleep. She thinks she recognizes the voice. She rubs her face and strains her eyes into the darkness.

"Nai Nai?" she asks to an empty room.

Outside is a beautiful, peaceful blackness. This is not the unfinished night of the city, it is complete. Stars spread throughout the sky, the appearance of longing.

———·———

S ANDY IS DEAD. That is what she has been told. And
is being told now. Mei lets the phone drift away
from her ear. The lawyer is still talking, settling up
Sandy's affairs. Putting his estate in order. She is standing in her apartment in her underwear in front of a
fan, blinds drawn, sweat rolling down the back of her
neck. A late August heatwave stagnates the city. Sandy
was the only relative she really had—blood relative,
that is. He had been an unstated constant in her life.
He had visited her frequently last summer, mostly out
of worry. He was right to, it was a hard season. She
doesn't want to talk to this lawyer now. She wants to
go back to imagining cold things. Icebergs. Winter. She
had seen Sandy last winter. It was the holidays and
they had smoked some mediocre weed and watched
stop-motion Christmas specials. Rudolph was Sandy's
favourite. She preferred the abominable snowman. He
called her a stick-in-the-mud.

"Who actually says stick-in-the-mud? You
sound so old!" She slapped the air in front of his face.

"I am many years older than you." He did
not blink.

"You even talk old. And you get less older than
me every year."

"What? What are you talking about?"

"Well. Like, the difference between someone
who's thirty and someone who's twenty-five is really different than the difference between twenty and
fifteen. Like, each year we actually get closer in age

because the percentage of our lives that has passed shrinks with each year. Like, when I was two, six months was like a quarter of my life! But, when I was twenty-four, six months was only ... um..."

Sandy stared blankly at her. She looked up from counting her fingers and stared back, hardly able to resist a smile.

Sandy, holding back, recognizing immediately that a staring contest had begun and he'd lost, burst into laughter. "Merry Christmas. You are cut off!"

"Are you aware of the property in Herbertsville?" A tinny voice pulls Mei back to the phone call with the lawyer. "Hello? ... Hello! Are you still there?"

Mei keeps losing herself in memories, coasting between ice floes. "Uh, yeah. Sorry."

"Well, as I was saying, Mr. Chow was quite specific: everything is left to you after debts are paid. There is a property in Herbertsville and his dog, Hazel, who's in a kennel right now. He left instructions about her. There is also the truck. Do you drive?"

"Yes. Yes, definitely." She drives, but unlicensed. She feels their conversation has no context. Their statements are unpunctuated words on white paper:

i can come by with the papers tomorrow if youd like
sure sounds fine   oh and uh sorry for your loss
thanks   see you tomorrow mr davis
miss   excuse me
miss davis   i dont follow
whatever ill see you tomorrow

W ITH THE DAYS shortening, Mei and Hazel both
need whatever daylight they can get. It is a task
for Mei to leave Bernadette and Sandy's bungalow. She
has been spending time in the cellar. The small staircase unfolds with a terrifying, exhilarating sound. The
wood sections slide freely, quicker than a staircase
should, only to be caught by a small metal shaft seconds before it would crash into the ground, destroyed.
The sharp smack of wood stopped by metal always excited Mei; as a child she could never predict when it
would happen. Now, older and alone, she knows when
the sound will come so precisely that she points to the
sky as the sections collide, a pantomime of mundane
magic she repeats each time she descends.

The cellar is vault-like, a square room that she
enters from the steep folding staircase. As Mei walks
down the stairs, a beaded metal chain brushes against
her shoulders. Tied to it is a red string that was once
intricately knotted with a turquoise piece of plastic
on the end so the light could be turned on and off
by people of any height standing in the centre of the
cellar. Sandy used it to frighten Mei when they were
children and she and her mother were visiting him and
Bernadette.

"Lemme show you something cool. It's in the
cellar." Sandy led Mei down the steep stairs. He pulled
the cord and turned the light on, illuminating the cellar until he reached the bottom and pulled on the cord
again, leaving Mei suspended, clinging to the stairs, an

abyss below, her eyes painfully adjusting to the afternoon light, suddenly bright, pouring through the trap door in the kitchen floor they had descended from. Sensing a prank coming, Mei defended herself by leaping into the darkness, fists up around her face ready for battle, like the Monkey King. Her elbow connected with Sandy's nose. Now, standing in the cellar alone, she inhales deeply, the smell of time filling her lungs. Back then, there had been no shelves full of labelled boxes, just canned food and potatoes.

Mei is going through the labelled boxes slowly, a box every couple of days. It passes the time and fills her in on missing family history. She also finds all of Bernadette's old clothes. She hasn't brought much with her to Herbertsville and she welcomes the discovery of a parka, extra sweaters, Sandy's ushanka, and blankets.

In one of the boxes Mei finds some of Sandy's school things: art he made as a child, drawings of houses, parents, families. He had trained his hands to create images that would fit. Mei picks up a drawing of the house, Bernadette, Sandy, and Jinhou, the dog they had before Hazel. The teacher had circled Jinhou's name and written *spelling?* underneath the word. Sandy had been so excited about Jinhou, about having a dog, but by the time Jinhou died, he was exhausted by having to explain his name to everyone they met. He had said the next dog he got would have a white name so he could get on with walking it.

There is also a journal in the box. She opens it, reading the first entry. There is no date:

Mom says she heard from someone on the radio that keeping a journal is good for boys cos it helps them learn about feelings and stuff but I think it's stupid. No one else I know has to keep a journal. I hate this. The end.

Mei thumbs through the pages; the journal is almost full. There are pages of shaky Chinese characters; Mei remembers that Nai Nai had been teaching Sandy how to write. "Pretty good for a kid who hates journaling," Mei says aloud. "I should get Connie to translate this—no, I should get her to *teach me* to translate this."

In another box marked with Chinese characters she does not recognize, she finds some of Nai Nai's embroidery. A phoenix and a dragon. A peach tree. Under the embroidery she finds a package of incense, decades old, and a small urn for burning it.

"This is definitely coming upstairs," she says, her eyes wide. She puts the journal in the box with characters on it and stacks it on top of the box of clothes. Arms full, she carefully makes her way upstairs. In the kitchen, she shuts the trap door to the cellar and covers it with a rug, out of sight.

After emerging from the cellar, Mei stands in the kitchen. The afternoon light is cutting long shadows through the house. The crumpled heart plant isn't doing any better in the kitchen, despite her diligent watering. She pulls Sandy's ushanka out of one of the boxes and puts it on.

"Oooh! You got one of those funny Russian hats with the earflaps!" She had teased him when he bought it.

"It's called an ushanka. What do they teach you in school?"

"I dunno, the same things they taught you in public school?" She had just started high school; Sandy had just finished college and had begun working maintaining the transfer station outside of Herbertsville.

She loves the Russian hat. The ushanka. It smells like the perfect mix of cigarettes, fast food, and machines. She keeps the earflaps of the hat down. Walking down the hall and into Sandy's room, she stands in front of his mirror; she sees Sandy's hat and Bernadette's huge wool sweater, her face lost amidst the fabric, a box of Nai Nai's things in her hands. She is locating herself in their things, her sense of self slowly reforming, cell by cell. She is a sapling growing from a fallen log.

Sandy's room is sparse. A bed, a dresser, a closet. On the dresser are two framed photos, one of Nai Nai and one of Bernadette and Hazel. Nai Nai is sitting in a wicker chair on the front porch of the house. She looks younger than Mei remembers her being. Her hair is mostly black and she wears it in a tight bun. She looks small in the chair, staring directly at the photographer, unsmiling. Mei had always thought it would be weird to live with your grandmother; none of the children who had lived in her neighbourhood lived with their grandmothers. Mei liked that she could visit all of her family at once but that she and her mother didn't have to live with them.

She puts down Nai Nai's box of things. She pulls out the urn and the incense. Running into the kitchen, holding Sandy's hat on her head with one hand and the urn in the other, she fills the small ceramic urn with soil from the dying plant. "Sorry little guy. I won't take any more," she promises, running back to Sandy's room.

She sets the urn in front of the pictures of Nai Nai and Bernadette. Using one of Sandy's lighters, she carefully lights a stick of incense. She has not done this since she was a small child. The fragrant smoke fills the house, awakening ghosts and calming her mind. She stands unmoving, watching the smoke curl from the small glowing ember. She raises the incense to her face and, holding it in front of her with arms outstretched, she bows from the waist three times. Nai Nai had taught her this. One bow for the heavens. One bow for the earth. One bow for the ancestors.

"Canadians do not care about old people," Nai Nai had said once, when Mei and her mother were visiting Herbertsville. They were in the wood-panelled kitchen with Bernadette, listening to Nai Nai. "They do not care. They send them away. Same way they do not care about dead people. Put them in the ground and forget." Nai Nai looked up from her embroidery, a fruiting peach tree, and stared coldly at Mei's mother. "Jun, why you live so far away? You leave me alone to die with this one." She moved her head slightly, gesturing to Bernadette, who exhaled, slowly embroidering something that had not yet taken shape.

"Your stitches are so big and clumsy!" Nai Nai said to Bernadette, who rolled her eyes and winked at Mei. She was going to nursing school and helping

Nai Nai in the restaurant. Recently, Nai Nai had agreed to close the restaurant on Mondays to give everyone a day off. The mother and her daughters were sitting around the table, and Sandy and Mei were in and out of the kitchen, playing around the tension. Enjoying a long weekend with each other. Nai Nai had managed to sit with her back to Bernadette, facing only Jun, though both of the daughters were beside her. She was ill, her illness slowly getting worse. Age, migration, and the steady battle against approaching poverty had taken their toll.

Jun looked at her exhausted sister, at her ten-year-old nephew, at his black eye and scraped arm. A fight at school. "Damn it, Ma! You're so dramatic! You can come live with us in the city any time you want. There are other Chinese people there. You'd have someone else to talk to," Jun urged, making exaggerated eye contact with her mother, knowing the coming response. It had been the same every time.

"Ahh. No, no. What do I do in the city? Your sister will wreck my restaurant. All my work! I cannot leave. Better you come stay with us, Jun. It will be good for Sandy. Be around a nicer boy, like Xiao Er."

Jun broke her gaze and poured a cup of tea.

"Xiao Er, lái." Nai Nai extended a hand, beckoning Mei over. Her hands were weathered, her knuckles swollen and round. The five-year-old crossed the kitchen and stood beside the old woman, who rubbed the child's head. "You so lovely. But you too soft. Jun, let Xiao Er stay here. With Sandy. Sandy will balance him." Her offer was more of a command.

"Sorry, Ma. I have to stay in the city. And go to work. At the job that gives me money. That I give to you." Jun's voice was calm, but her hand shook slightly as she raised her tea cup to drink.

"You not working now."

"Ma! It's a holiday!"

"This why you don't keep husband. You too proud." Nai Nai was still rubbing Mei's head.

Bernadette's eyebrows rose.

Jun's face darkened. "What did you say?" Each word was hard, the head of a hammer tapping the palm of a hand.

Bernadette smiled and shook her head, laughing, breaking the fragile tension in the room. "You never ask me why I can't keep a man!" she grinned.

"That's not funny, jiejie." Jun's words were hushed, her disdain barely contained.

Nai Nai fiercely whispered, "Zhù kǒu! Xiǎo hái zi zài zhè! Shut your mouth. The children are here."

Bernadette's grin disappeared. For a moment nothing was said. Nai Nai broke the silence with a cough.

Bernadette got up from the table and called for Sandy's dog: "Jinhou! Lái! We're going for a walk."

The young Mei, still standing beside Nai Nai, did not know what had occurred. Nai Nai gently pushed the child over to Sandy, who stood in the doorway between the kitchen and the living room.

"Zǒu bā! Go outside with Sandy," Nai Nai said.

Sandy's face dropped in disappointment. "Oh, c'mon!" he protested, but took Mei by the hand out to the backyard.

"Why don't you want to go outside, Sandy?"

"You really have no idea what's going on, do you?" He shook his head, ripping the leaves off a low-hanging branch as he walked past.

———·———

"XIAO MEI! XIAO MEI! Why are you lying on the floor like that? Gào su wǒ." The voice startles her awake. This is not part of the plan. Mei was supposed to get drunk, stop being a wimp about things, take all of the Valium she'd bought ages ago, all of the Tylenol 3s she'd taken from Sandy's place over the years, and be done with this.

Sandy's been dead a week. She has not gone to pick up the keys to his house in Herbertsville, but she has managed to get Hazel, the dog, down to her place in the city. She is tired—no, exhausted. By what, she can't remember anymore. Getting attacked last summer. Sandy dying this summer. Sandy being dead. The constant search for community or retreat from it. What seems like a never-ending run of "almosts" or "not-at-alls." That, and being lonely and broke. But she isn't supposed to be running through lists of reasons why she is lying here—one more "almost" to add to the list.

She is, however, all the way lying in her own vomit. Nothing almost about this situation. She pulls her face away from the acrid smell, nauseous. She hasn't cleaned the bathroom in years. She is sprawled out on the pleasantly cool tiles, head pounding and the voice of her dead Nai Nai echoing around her. The tiles are white and set in a black grout, which she notices for the first time. The contrast is stark and gives her the impression she is somehow represented on a graph. Her dizzy mind flashes back to two awful semesters at the University of Dundurn. First year general sciences, her mother had insisted. What is the line of best fit for a puddle of vomit? What axis is she even working with? Mei can't remember; she had only stayed until the end of that first year—almost to the end of that first year. The only class she had liked was meteorology, but mostly she liked to drink coffee and listen to the professor. Unfortunately she was not tested on his use of metaphor.

Nai Nai's voice comes again, interrupting her remembrance, grating in her ears. Nai Nai is actually speaking quite gently, but the cheap whiskey she'd been drinking makes sure she hears every tone very clearly. Too clearly. She moves her head quickly, looking to see where the voice is coming from, and sends the room spinning. She cannot place what is happening. She could be hallucinating. It's not likely. She has not taken the right combination of things for that. Maybe she is dreaming. Whatever is swirling around in her system could give lucid dreams. She wonders, assuming she survives the night, if she could market this new lucid dreaming skill she's found. She is thinking about where she will fly in this dream when Nai Nai sucks her teeth. It sounds like someone ripping the wings off a starling. Mei winces.

"Aiya! Xiao Mei! Get off the floor."

Mei decides it would be best to engage. "Yeah I know, Nai Nai. I really should clean it." As Mei sits up, wiping her mouth with her hand, Nai Nai sucks her teeth again. "Whatever, it's not like I haven't got puke all over me anyways, and just because I can't see you doesn't mean I can't hear you looking at the floor like that. I've been ... busy."

"Xiao Mei! Nǐ zuì jìn bù máng le. You not busy! You depressed!"

Ashamed for lying, Mei says nothing. What is Mei doing here? Sandy is dead, but it isn't like he was the only person she ever hung out with. She just can't seem to shake the crushing loneliness his death brought. He'd left her a house, a dog, and a truck she definitely cannot afford. And now she is talking to ghosts in a dirty bathroom. Clearly this reaction is not about Sandy entirely. *No matter how you frame it, talking to ghosts makes you sound crazy*, Mei thinks.

"Fēng le mǎ? Wǒ lái bāng nǐ shì fēng le mǎ? Crazy? I come help you is crazy? You know what crazy? Nǐ kàn diàn shì tài duō le! Looking at the little screen all the time! Fēng le!"

"I don't watch too much TV! It's too hot outside."

"Bú duì! Xiao Mei, you watch too much TV. Why else would I come?"

Mei is half sitting up, leaning against the bathtub.

"You not healthy, Mei. You need to change the scene."

Mei's face contorts in confusion as Nai Nai's voice seems to change to a howl, and the room fills with the sound of scratching and clawing. She gasps and sits up fully. Hazel is howling at the locked door of the bathroom.

"Hazel! Aiya, shut up!"

Hazel whines and walks away from the door, her claws clicking down the hallway on her way back to the bedroom. There is vomit all over the floor, a protest against the perfectly arranged squares, empty bottle and scattered pills across her body. Looking around, she decides she must have passed out next to the bathtub and puked beside the toilet. Standing up, she falters, remembering the dream. After she has cleaned the floor, she exits the bathroom. This isn't how she had planned on leaving it.

ɔ

Later that night, in her bed with Hazel, she dreams that the only line is the horizon between the water and the sky.

———■———

THE WINTER SHOULD be over soon. The sun wakes her through the windows earlier each day, cutting into her sleep. The cold and the snow don't seem ready to leave Herbertsville. Mei, tired of feeling sequestered in the house, heads into town. In Herbertsville, like so many towns away from the cities to the south, there is an area where the shops happen: banks in the centre, small stores fanning out from there. Herbertsville Presbyterian Church runs a thrift store on Saturdays; Mei had seen the flyer in the grocery store the last time she was buying food and made a plan to visit.

Mei walks through the main entrance to the church, then follows the signs up old stairs, dulled by years of bleach-covered mops and thousands of steps. Melting snow, left from boots up and down the stairs, has evaporated, leaving white outlines, dried lakes. A yellow light at the top of the stairs drifts over enormous cork boards, which are covered in community announcements: A bake sale. A pageant. A choir. Someone who has come back from doing mission work abroad is going to give a presentation next Sunday after worship. Coffee will be provided; food is potluck.

Mei walks down a hallway between a series of doors. So far she has not seen anyone, but the rooms off the hallway are full of things: A room of pants and shoes. A room of coats and winter clothes. A room of books. She has found the Herbertsville Presbyterian Thrift Store. She wanders into the last room and lets herself get lost.

There are rows of books behind rows of
books. She digs through them, excavating the tastes
and curiosities of Herbertsville's residents, the ideas
they don't need anymore. Mei wonders if she'll find
any of Bernadette's things here but knows it's not likely. Everything she had, she seems to have catalogued
and ordered meticulously in the cellar. Behind one of
the piles of books is a stack of old suitcases. Leaning
down, Mei starts opening them and examining the
musty luggage. Some still have address tags from ocean
liners—*If found, return to: Blue Bird Liners.* They have
beautifully weathered sides. She opens one that has
been set down beside the pile. A recent addition. It is
stunning. A crimson velvet lines the black case, so soft
and padded, the inside bottom rounded with the fabric. The interior is ringed by pockets with loose red
velvet elastics. There are two bands that make an 'X'
inside the lid of the case.

"Hello? Do I have a customer?" comes a voice
from another room, followed by footsteps. "Good
morning! Did you find something?" An older man with
greying hair steps into the book room and looks over
to Mei, his hands deep in the pockets of a thick brown
wool cardigan. "Oh! You found something! Excellent.
That just came in. Poor man just passed away. Used to
come to service from time to time. More than Christmas
and Easter, but not too much more, mind you. His
name started with an 'N,' Nicholas was it? Maybe it was
Nathan. My memory it isn't wh—" the man interrupts
himself with a sneeze. "It is ever so dusty here. Not to
worry!" He reaches into forest green corduroys, pulls

out a handkerchief, and wipes his nose.

"It's lovely," Mei says, not sure how to respond.

The older man gives her a quick smile followed by a brief, questioning look.

"The case. The case is lovely," she clarifies.

"Certainly not my handkerchief!" he laughs, then takes the case in his hand. "It is, isn't it? Two dollars sound like a fair price to you ... Miss?"

"Uh, yes, definitely," she manages, unsure whether or not he is only asking about a price.

"Excellent. You can pay me on your way out." Turning away, the man leaves Mei surrounded by books.

She spends the rest of the afternoon flipping through paperbacks and brittle magazines piled on the cracking linoleum.

———·———

S ANDY AND BERNADETTE'S place is close enough to town that Mei can walk to the small grocery store. The errand gets her out of the house and provides a good walk for Hazel. The winter is finally breaking, receding. Melting snow darkens the soil. Mei would describe the grocery store as being in a small strip mall, knowing the words suggest a larger area than it is in reality. There is a small parking lot for the grocery store, the pharmacy, and a bar. Metal poles painted a rusty brown unevenly hold up an awning covering the sidewalk. Down the road, after a small collection of houses and two churches, is the centre of town.

Mei ties up Hazel outside the grocery store and walks in. Once inside, she peeks through the window to check on the dog. She sees a woman in a plaid coat, a bit older than her mother would be now, saying hello to Hazel. Mei smiles at how friendly Hazel is with strangers. On one of their first trips into the grocery store, there had been a thin man, older as well, saying hello to Hazel. He had noticed Mei checking on Hazel through the front window and stared back at her an instant longer than was comfortable, taking all of her in. It was an unsettling stare, but Mei had felt no hostility from him; he appeared struck by some sad recognition. The whole time, Hazel's tail was wagging like she was standing with family.

ɔ

"Hey! You! You staying at Bernie's place?" demands a voice from behind her in the grocery store.

She doesn't turn around; no one would be looking for her here. She looks in the basket. A bag of rice, some lentils. Apples. Ginger. She is looking for garlic.

"Hey!" The voice comes again—not angry, almost excited. Whoever the voice belongs to is persistent.

She had been surprised when she got to town and found the grocery store had hummus and hoisin sauce. But she had immediately felt her cheeks get hot with embarrassment, knowing she'd been too long in the city. Of course they had hummus and hoisin. She just hadn't been in this grocery store since the nineties, when people still used answering machines with little tapes.

"HEY!" The voice is right behind her now. She turns around and sees a woman, older than her, smiling at Mei as though they had gone to high school together. Her enthusiasm is unfamiliar to Mei. Even Annette doesn't get this excited to see her. The woman is wearing a dirty plaid coat and a white shirt with a flamingo on it. It is the woman who said hello to Hazel minutes earlier, and she is looking for Mei.

"You're staying at Bernie's old place!" It is not a question, as it turns out. The flamingo woman knows exactly where Mei is staying.

"Uh. Yeah. Bernadette was my aunt." Mei looks quizzically at her.

The woman is wearing sandals and cargo shorts. Mei is wearing two of Sandy's sweaters, a jacket, pants, and boots. And a scarf. Looking around the store, she notices that no one else is as bundled as she is. *The overly padded transsexual and the flamingo woman*, Mei thinks.

"You alright? You look a bit sour. Got a cold?" The woman looks concerned.

"No ... sorry. Yeah, uh, Aunt Bernadette. I'm staying at her place," Mei tries again.

"Well, how about that! Bernie was a close friend of mine. I miss her every day. Sandy too. My condolences. Name's Diane. How long you around for?" Diane extends her hand and firmly shakes Mei's arm.

"Thanks. I dunno. A few months I guess. I wanted to get out of the city."

"Fair enough. Bit shy are ya? That's okay." Then she whispers, conspiring with Mei, "It must be weird having your dead aunt's girlfriend chase you down in the store." She raises her voice slightly, having conveyed the sensitive information. "What should I call you?"

"My what? Aunt Bernadette's what?" Mei lets out, too loudly for Diane.

"Hey now, not so loud. Honey, you don't look like you'd be surprised." Diane's hands partially extend, as she tries very hard not to blow their cover in the store. "Surely you must have known, I mean, *look at you*," she whispers again, winking. "You look like you have a toaster or two yourself! So what's your name?"

Mei pauses. "My name is Mei ... sorry. A toaster?"

Diane's forehead gently wrinkles and she smiles at Mei. "I suppose you are pretty young. Well, uh, nice to meet you. What was your name again?"

"It's Mei."

"Great! Well, *Mei,* how'd you get here? Can I give you a lift back? Is that Sandy's dog outside? Which one is that, Hazel? I've seen her before around here." Diane gestures to the front of the store with her chin. "I think my buddy Nelson was talking about seeing her."

ɔ

At the checkout, the cashier smiles at Mei. "Hello dear," she says. "Did you find everything today?"

Mei hasn't seen her before, despite coming here each week. "Yes, thank you." Mei pulls out her wallet.

The cashier, beaming, continues: "I got a niece—I mean a nephew—like you. Lives out west now."

Mei, startled, stares blankly.

"I just think it's great, people like him. And you. Brave enough to do what you're doing." Giving Mei an earnest look, she puts her hand on her vest to show Mei a tiny rainbow button. "Look, see?"

Stunned, Mei smiles reticently at the cashier as she scratches the back of her hand and nods, noticing other customers staring. A few smile and one scowls. Mei tries to quickly remember if she'd always come to the grocery store on the same day of the week and had suddenly broken her routine, but she hasn't paid attention to the date in months.

"We'll see you again, dear," the cashier assures her.

Mei's face flushes. These interactions feel like a mix of coffee and booze, the warmth of recognition and the anxiety of direct attention. She is unsettled by the host of uncertainties that comes with being recognized as a trans woman by a room full of strangers. Besides, rainbows make Mei feel buried, lost. Why is support so rarely uncomplicated, she wonders, her scarf falling from around her neck as she walks, arms full, to meet Diane waiting by the exit.

"You ready?"

"Uh, yeah. Yeah. Ready."

Diane straightens her shoulders and her forehead wrinkles again.

"She was just being nice. You gotta get better at taking a compliment."

Mei looks at Diane, wondering about this new person, and at their inexperienced alliance.

"I mean, you almost look insulted," Diane adds.

"I'm just a bit confused. Just thinking." Mei tries to place Diane, an older white woman, confidently walking out of the store to her truck. She asks her, "Do you ever find that acceptance isn't as simple as you'd like it to be?"

"Nope." Diane pauses. "Well, sometimes. But generally, nope."

ɔ

Diane drives a green Chrysler pickup with a bench seat. Hazel rides in the bed, and Mei, sitting in the cab, finds her feet hardly even touch the floor. Her mom never had trucks; she only ever rode in them when she came out to see Bernadette and Sandy. In the truck, watching the fields pass, riding out to the house from town, Mei realizes she hasn't let herself arrive here yet. She's been stuck in her head all winter, as though afraid. She's had occasional calls from Annette and long conversations with Hazel, but nothing else. But here in the truck, the road bumping them now and again, seeing the fences blur like a painted line across the landscape, she feels herself relax. She feels like she'll get to the house and Sandy and Bernadette will be there.

"So, what are you doing up in these parts?" Diane asks, cutting the silence.

"Dog-sitting," Mei says, flatly, still looking out the window, her eyes drinking in the new green of spring breaking through the muddy brown remnants of snow drifts.

Diane clears her throat. "I'm sorry about Sandy. It was a shock. Helped raised him but I hadn't seen him in years."

Leaning back in the seat, Mei makes room for the statement. "How come I never met you before? My aunt died when I was a teenager. I thought she had a husband. Sandy's dad. No one ever talked about him though. I just figured he was an asshole and it was good he wasn't around."

"I guess I could be an asshole sometimes," Diane admits, grinning. "But Bernie didn't like me around when family was up. Man oh man, did we ever fight about that. But ultimately it was her house. We debated about whose family it was. But it was her house, and I had one of my own, so I respected that. Mostly. I would leave when you came round; I have a place one concession over. You must be Jun's kid. Bernie and I used to place bets on how you'd turn out. 'Course I never met you, but based on what she said, well. We figured you were gonna be on our team one way or another. Looks like Bernie was right." Her hands drift on the steering wheel; she looks idly around her, as though she's comfortable in the role of elder, or at least the presentation of it.

"What do you keep hinting at?" Mei is looking directly at Diane, watching her face, a fuzzy bud of her family history breaking the soil.

Diane slowly shakes her head and for a moment looks at the steering wheel. "You really have no idea?"

"No idea about what?"

"After all those visits—which she loved, by the way. Her helping you with your hair..." Diane's voice shifts from its monotone range.

"Okay. It's creepy how you know all this stuff about me. What are you talking about?"

"Sandy never told you? Not once?"

"Told me what?" Mei's voice is on the verge of rising. Who is this woman who appears to know everything about her?

"Bernie, dear Mei, was my lover. Well, in an on-again, off-again kind of way. It—it was complicated," Diane stumbles. "But as my lover, well, she told me all about you and your family."

"So? I don't tell most of the people I sleep with a thing about my family. Aunt Bernadette was gay..." Mei mumbles in disbelief. This hadn't quite set in when Diane brought it up in the grocery store.

"At least with me she was," Diane grins, returning Mei's gaze, then looking out the window and not saying anything for long enough that the silence is noticeable. "And she told me all about you." Mei doesn't know if she should be angry or astonished.

Diane drives them past the railroad tracks on the west side of the town. For a moment, just as the truck is in the centre of the tracks, Mei catches a glimpse of what looks like an infinite straight line, shooting off, every railroad tie briefly visible at once. Beside the tracks there is a long flat shoulder, wide enough to be a road.

"A friend of mine died there this past winter. My buddy, Nelson Hendricks. The one I was telling you about, who loved dogs. I used to see him at Dale's Grill all the time, the bar over there by the grocery store. Everyone said he had a heart attack sitting in his car watching the trains from the side of the road. He froze and died," Diane tells Mei, quietly. "I don't know what I think about it."

"That's really sad."

"Yeah, it is." She turns and smiles, her eyes focussing on something behind Mei's head. They are almost at the house. "Well, here we are," Diane says, pulling in and putting the truck in park. "You need a hand with the groceries?"

"Nah, I got it. Thanks for the ride."

Diane pauses before turning the truck off, about to say something, her eyes almost glassy. "You know, you really look a lot like him. Like Sandy."

Mei sits half on the seat facing her, hand on the door handle, unsure of how to react. The air in the truck halts, suspended around Diane for an instant. She exhales loudly.

"Anyway, if you ever need anything you call me." Diane breathes sharply and reaches across Mei into the glove box. She pulls out a pen and paper and writes down a number. "It's my cell. Give me a shout whenever."

"Hey Diane, do you know where I could get one of those tapes for the answering machine?"

"What? You still use that? Don't you have a cell phone or something?"

Mei stares at Diane, silent for a moment before responding, "People keep telling me that. Never mind. Hey, thanks for the lift. It was great to meet you."

"You too!"

Mei gets out of the truck, opens the tailgate for Hazel, and they walk toward the house. Mei stops and turns, the gravel driveway grinding beneath her feet.

"You wanna come by for dinner sometime? I'll cook for you."

Diane chuckles. "Sure, I'd love that. Give me a shout when you want company." She waves, backing out onto the concession.

Mei waves back and nods, walking back into the house. She wonders why Sandy had never talked about her, why he hadn't mentioned how queer their family really was. Once inside she puts the groceries on the kitchen table and fills the kettle with water. She tries to remember anything that Sandy might have said to suggest that Diane even existed. Anything to suggest that Bernadette was gay. She idly turns the crumpled heart plant, stopping suddenly, noticing new growth. The green is brilliant against the pale brown of the dead leaves. The kettle boils. Taking the tea to the living room, she picks up the phone and dials.

"Annette? I met a woodsy dyke."

"I knew it! I knew it! Tell me everything."

"Well, she's my Aunt Bernadette's girlfriend."

"Aunt Bernadette was gay?"

————·———

MEI IS ROOTING through the house, looking for candles and wine glasses. At least that's why she started opening boxes, but with so many lining the walls of the basement, she is easily distracted. Sandy didn't get rid of anything when his mother died. He didn't have to. Bernadette's organization of the house meant that when she passed, nothing had to be dealt with.

Standing in the cellar, Mei looks around at the boxes marked with years and names. She opens the most recent *Bernadette* box. It is light, holding only a quilt, the perfect size for a small child. It looks as though it was sewn by hand. On the front is an embroidered goose, flying in a thunderstorm. "Weird. This is definitely coming upstairs," Mei says. She decides she'll never find wine glasses down here. Diane is coming over for dinner in a couple of hours. Mei figures that she doesn't care about things like wine glasses and probably only drinks beer anyway.

ɔ

Mei hears a truck pull into the driveway from the kitchen and assumes it is Diane. She keeps preparing things for their meal, expecting to hear the truck door slam and Diane knocking at the door. After a few minutes she realizes she hasn't heard either of those sounds, and she walks to the front door and looks out the window. Diane is sitting in the truck, staring at the house. Mei can see the solitary goose she's been seeing all winter standing on the lawn, watching the truck. Noticing Mei, Diane gives a wave and gets out of the truck. She steps onto the driveway and the goose seems to move toward her. Mei watches, curious about what is unfolding. The goose is definitely staring at Diane, not the backpack in her hand, and walking toward her. Its head tilts slowly from side to side, as if taking in as many angles of her as it can with its small black eyes. The bird, advancing, starts to hiss. Diane, moving slowly, takes a step back toward the truck as the goose charges. She leans down and yells something; Mei can't hear the words through the door. Diane, still leaning down and staring at the goose, doesn't move quickly enough to dodge its lunge at her face, and it catches her cheek with its beak. Mei throws open the front door and runs at the goose. It stops its attack and looks at Mei before turning its back to the two women and walking away.

"What was that about? You make fun of his mother?" Mei laughs.

Diane says nothing, just stares at the ground.

"You okay, Diane?" Mei asks, moving toward her.

Diane nods.

"Let's go in," Mei says. She enters the house first, then turns to see Diane standing in the doorway, hesitating.

Diane takes a deep breath. "I'm coming. I'm coming."

"You sure you're okay?" Mei asks, offering Diane a wet towel. The goose didn't break the skin on her face, but its beak has left a small mark. The two of them walk into the kitchen. Diane stands awkwardly by the table holding the towel to her face. Mei pulls out a chair and gestures to it, inviting Diane to sit down. Mei offers her some tea.

"Nah, I brought wine. It's in my bag, you wanna open it for me? I'd love a drink."

Mei opens the wine and pours some in a plastic juice glass.

"You don't know where the wine glasses are, do ya?" Diane scoffs. "Honestly, Bernie would have a fit if she saw you serving me wine in a juice cup."

"I tried to find some before you came, but I don't even remember Aunt Bernadette having wine glasses, or wine in the house."

Laughing, Diane walks over to a cupboard, puts one knee on the counter, and hoists herself up. "They're up here, Mei. Behind the measuring cups. Don't ask me why. Like I said, she had her house and I had mine."

Mei is stunned. Neither she nor Sandy would have ever dreamed of climbing on the counter like that. Nai Nai and, later, Bernadette would have made them clean the counter, the floor, the cupboards, the kitchen walls, the fridge. Everything. "What are you doing? You can't be up there!" Mei blurts out.

Diane turns to her. "Look at you. Standing in her kitchen, wearing her sweater. Of course you weren't allowed up here. That's where we kept the pot." Diane jumps down from the counter, wine glass in hand, pours the contents of her juice cup into the glass, and takes a sip, immediately gagging. "I should have dusted that," she says, touching her throat. "That's what I get for showing off."

"So, what's a guy like you doing out here? I mean, don't you got a boyfriend or something at home? This ain't exactly San Francisco." Diane is sitting across the kitchen table from Mei, cutting through the frozen lasagne Mei had heated up for them. A piece balances on the end of her fork, which Diane idly pops into her mouth, continuing to speak, her mouth full. "You really stand out. Why, I'm surprised no one told me a guy like you was hanging around here!"

Mei has finished eating and is slowly drinking the wine Diane brought. Diane is at home in the space. From what Diane has said over the course of the evening, she used to spend a lot of time in the house. After revealing where the wine glasses were kept, she helped Mei find some candles in the back of the third drawer beside the stove. She has brought a couple of bottles of wine and is drinking most of them. There has been little silence between the two of them, the conversation topics moving organically, unselfconsciously. Mei is surprised to find herself talking openly with Diane. She feels like family, the good kind of family. Since she last spent time with Sandy, she hasn't started to feel like someone knows a bit about her, or acknowledges anything beyond what she tells them. That feeling of familiarity is almost as jarring as Diane's latest comment. Mei quickly scans her memory, trying to remember their conversations. There has been no need to correct an introduction, but how has Mei said nothing about who she is? Surely after how much Bernadette seems to have told Diane about Mei, how close they were, she would have known this. Mei just assumed that Diane knew she was trans.

"You mean, what's a girl like me doing here?" Mei corrects Diane.

"Yeah, sure. *Mary*." Diane leans in and winks. "There's a couple of gay guys I know a few towns over. Real *queens*." She winks again.

Mei rubs her face with her hands, and pours herself another glass of wine. "Aunt Bernadette didn't tell you I'm trans?"

"Yeah, a transvestite, right? Like a drag queen." Diane is taking another piece of lasagne.

"Not quite. Like a transsexual. Like a trans woman. You know, a woman, not a man."

Mei is racing through their conversations now, trying to remember if any pronouns have been used. Did Mei say something that would suggest she was a man? The interaction with the cashier, Diane had heard that. She has only talked about Sandy and Bernadette. Mei tries to locate where she has misled Diane, recalls nothing, and is instantly ashamed that she would blame herself before Diane's assumptions.

"What do you mean?" Diane's left eyebrow raises as she cuts the lasagne with her fork, scraping the plate. "You're the gay nephew. You're really into all those gay rock musicians from the seventies."

Mei's mouth is open. "No, I'm the trans *niece*. I'm a lady. As in not a man. Not the gay nephew. The gay *niece*."

Diane stares at Mei for a long second, as if holding Mei's words between them, turning them, scrutinizing them. "You think you're a girl?" Diane says, slowly. Each word is enunciated.

"I know I am. People call me she. I use the women's washroom ... I get sexually harassed on the street ... Men treat me like I don't know what I'm doing, especially when they think they're being nice ... A woman. I date gay ladies, sometimes guys, not so much anymore, but that's beside the point. Gay ladies date me because they also date gay ladies ... like me."

Diane has put down her fork. A piece of lasagne is partially cut on her plate. Her face has changed. The free-flowing humour and well-practiced arrogance that was restrained enough to be charming is gone. She is stoic.

"You take those pills?" she asks.

Mei can't believe this is happening. Bernadette's sweater is heavy, like a blanket on her shoulders. She sees the table, Diane, the wine as if they are a panoramic photograph.

"Hormones? I use a patch, actually," Mei hears herself answering.

"You, ah, got your, you know..." Diane looks in front of Mei as if looking at her crotch through the tabletop. Her lips are tight.

Mei's eyes widen and she says nothing.

"Whatever. It doesn't matter anyway. I get it. I know about guys like you. I used to work weekends at this women's shelter a few towns over. We had a couple of ... you, trying to stay in the space with the women."

Mei watches the conversation change. She is pulling back from her body, her skin getting further away.

"And we didn't let them." Diane stares directly into Mei's eyes. "I like you, kid," Diane continues, without breaking her gaze. "Sandy must have too. I'm hoping you're just confused."

Mei sees the table, the remains of dinner. Bits of tomato sauce drying on her plate. She'll have to let everything soak before she scrubs it. She'll have to work a bit to get the plates clean, and she really doesn't want to clean the aluminum pan the lasagne was in— noodles have gathered in the tight folds at the corners of the tray. This is, of course, unavoidable; there is no way to remove lasagne perfectly from this kind of tray, as nothing fits the tight confusing folds properly, and the aluminum won't let go easily. The tray will have to be flooded to get the noodles out. Even though she has many cooking dishes in the house, she feels she can't afford to waste them. *This is what happens when you don't make the lasagne from scratch in a proper pan*, she thinks, remembering Bernadette, a Chinese woman far from home, telling her how to make lasagne properly.

That conversation had been at this table, too. Looking back at the lasagne pan, she thinks about just throwing the whole thing in the garbage. She is going to clean the pan. She knows she will. Not out of a belief in recycling, but out of fear that if she doesn't, all of her favourite cartoon characters will get together, somewhere, and cry, their public service lessons wasted on the children of the nineties. But first, she should respond to Diane. She is the only person she knows in Herbertsville and the only person she's spoken to face to face in months. But she can't find the right response.

How could I have let my guard down? And why am I reacting like this? This isn't a date! Mei thinks, watching Diane, dissecting their conversation. Measuring questions against responses, testing the weight of their statements.

"Like I said, I like ya." Diane gives Mei a firm stare. "But you have no idea what you're talking about. You can't just go ahead and make a woman." She looks closely at Mei, who meets her gaze for an instant and then looks at Hazel, asleep at her feet. "Well, I'm gonna get going. Thanks for the food. You need anything, you call me. I'll see ya around." Diane stands up, leaving the dishes.

Mei manages to mumble, "Yeah. See ya."

Diane lets herself out. The sun has set, leaving the candles on the table quietly burning, the only light. The orange flicker throws shadows about the room, filling the empty space with silhouettes.

——— · ———

"DAMN IT, SANDY!" It is autumn. Mei is furious. He had been trying to protect her again, and not in any way she had asked for. She knew Sandy was expecting her call and would have a barely acceptable logic about how "the guy had it coming." Of course Mei agreed; she had dated "the guy who had it coming" for nearly a year. But she never expected Sandy would run into him. It is three years after Bernadette died, and Sandy is working maintaining electrical substations.

"I told you I didn't need your help, Sandy! It was fine. I had already dealt with it! I am more than capable of dealing with my own problems." She is standing in the middle of her apartment, one hand holding the phone to her ear, the other flying around her, emphasizing each word: "I've been living on my own for years, just fine. Then you decide you wanna pull an urban cowboy or something and start driving into town and beating up my exes! I told him to leave me alone and he did. I *dealt* with it."

"You think you dealt with it, but really—"

"Do *not* even start with that, Sandy!"

"I didn't drive into town just to beat—"

"Then what were you doing here?" She knows her accusation makes little sense. He had gone to college in the city; he had friends here.

"I was visiting some of the guys from school. Mei, you're only a kid! He wasn't taking you seriously."

She straightens her back as she hears this. She can hardly believe the argument they are having.

"It sounds like he wasn't the only one not taking me seriously!"

Sandy exhales slowly. She imagines him running his hand through his hair, cornered.

"Sorry," he says. "You're totally right. I just thought—"

"Ugh! That is not an apology. It's turning into an excuse."

"No, it's just that—"

"I know, I know. Her dying wish was for you to protect me because somehow she knew that I was gonna be some weak little gay boy or turn out to—tada—be a girl, so I needed your big man protection. Get a girlfriend." Mei pauses. "Sorry. That was too far. But seriously, don't beat anyone else up for me. It's not really for me anyways and you know it. You get something out of it. I think it's mostly for you." Her voice has softened.

"You're right, Mei. I won't do it again. I hated the way he was talking about you. I didn't even mean to find him. He was just spouting off about you in that bar, and, well ... yeah. Sorry."

"How did you even know it was him? Also it was weeks ago! Why didn't you tell me?"

"He was just being so loud, talking about some half-breed shemale. He was pretty wasted. It was hard not to hear him. I asked him a couple of questions—well, one, and yeah ... it was him. Sorry."

Mei, sighing, relaxes. "Okay. I'm glad you're around. You don't need a girlfriend. Or maybe you do. I don't know. Maybe you need a boyfriend..." She smiles.

"Nice try. That is not what I'm after."

Mei walks to her fridge and opens it, absently perusing. "Annette could find you a man in no time," she goads.

"Annette, she's your friend you told me about? When you gonna introduce us?"

"That is never, never going to happen."

"Never say never. I have tomorrow off. I could drive into the city and have breakfast with you if you want."

Mei laughs. "Sure."

The next morning at breakfast, Sandy can't resist: "So what did you do to your ex? How was it 'dealt with'?" He smirks, sipping his coffee.

Mei puts a potato in her mouth, chewing it slowly, carefully swallowing before responding. "Don't be condescending. Just because I didn't break his nose doesn't mean I didn't get back at him."

"So what did you do?"

Mei sips her coffee. "First I gave his mailing address and email to all of the porn sites I could think of, and then I just started signing him up for mailing lists."

Sandy leans back in the booth, shrugging his shoulders. The puffy vinyl on the back of the booth deflates.

Mei ignores him. "Things like *Reader's Digest*, *Watchtower*, some scientology thing, everything. But instead of putting his name as the addressee, I put a nickname his mom used to call him that I always made fun of."

Sandy's eyebrows raise. He adds a creamer to his coffee and stirs it absently.

"Can you stop?" Mei is exasperated. "He hated it, I know it. I did it so he would know it was me. He hates junk mail. Hates it. That was the first thing."

"Thank god it wasn't the only thing. Junk mail? *Junk mail* is your idea of revenge?"

Mei stabs another potato with her fork, and the plate clinks in protest. "No. Well, kind of."

Sandy laughs.

"But then—then!" Mei continues. "Then, I still had his key, you see, so I went into his apartment when I knew he was at work and I took back all my records, put tea bags in his shower head, switched his salt for sugar, put plastic wrap on the toilet seat and red food colouring in his milk." She checks off each action with a tap of the potato on the end of her fork. "I debated breaking the key off in his lock, but decided that was too far. I sent the key back to him with a Christmas card a few months later. I covered the key in table syrup."

Sandy's displeasure has made way for an open-mouthed smile.

"I mean, seriously," Mei continues, "he tells me he can't introduce me to his family because they wouldn't like him dating a man, and then I find him in bed with an actual man a week later. Who he'd been dating for a month! I could care less if he sleeps around, I just wanna know. We were having unprotected sex!"

Sandy shakes his head. "I guess I didn't need to break his nose."

Mei glares. "No, you didn't. It wasn't your place. You just wanted to punch someone and I happen to have a jerk ex-boyfriend who was laughing about me with his friends. You used me." She sits back in the booth and looks out the window, the fork she is holding resting against her tightly pursed lips.

The morning sun is slipping in the windows of the diner through thin curtains. There are sounds of grilling, service bells, and coffee makers gurgling. The city wakes around them.

Suspended in between the lake and the sky, she thinks of diagrams she has seen of stars displacing space-time. They remind her of a blanket on a lawn that someone has dropped a bowling ball onto. Tonight, she is that bowling ball, warping the lake. Her mass ripples the meeting of water and air. She tries to imagine what a scream would look like extending from her now, continuous in all directions.

All the movement around her, the movement that comes from her presence in the lake, makes her feel better about being so self-centred. Since Sandy died, she is rarely out of her head long enough to maintain an in-person conversation. Phone calls are different. The physical absence of the other person creates a feeling of safety. No eyes to scan for reactions, no revealing hand movements. Just a sound.

Now she is in the boat in the bay wondering if she could find herself or the shore if the sky clouded over. No facial expressions, no sounds other than her stolen paddle breaking the surface of the bay. The water, reflecting the sky, holds the stars, wavering points of light that outline the boat, her arms. Without these pinholes, what would she reference herself against? A change in weather and she would lose her position. She would not be able to guide herself or anyone else.

KINGDOM OF BRIDGES

I T IS A warm night. She can get away without wearing a sweater. Mei returned to the city last week from a few days visiting Sandy up in Herbertsville; it is still strange to visit and not see Bernadette. Mei is walking to the bus stop lightly drunk after leaving the bar. She tired early and left before everyone else. Annette wasn't about leave; she'd gotten the attention of a man visiting from New York who kept buying her drinks and making bad jokes about sports teams. Annette laughed at each one of them, putting her hand on his shoulders and playing with his hair. He was cute, but Mei can watch straight people flirt whenever she wants to just by turning on her TV.

"You're such a grump, Mei!" Annette said in the bathroom before she left. "Steven's so nice. And *handsome*! You can go if you want, I got a brick and mace in my purse. I can take him. His shoulders are nice but they're not all that big." Annette was teasing Mei. "I hope he gives good head."

"Ugh! Don't wanna hear it."

"Whatever, slut shamer. Didn't you go to some workshop on that? Positivity sex or something?"

"Sex positivity," Mei rolled her eyes, turning on the tap.

"That's it, I knew it was something you'd learned

from one of those white girls with plastic glasses and septum piercings." Annette ran her tongue over her teeth, loosening a forgotten piece of food before picking something out of her eye, then looked at Mei in the mirror.

"Whatever, Annette, I hope he gives good head and finds your prostate with his thick hands. Get him to use lots of lube. And if you ever came to one of those workshops you'd see it's not just white queer women."

"Whoa. Defensive much?"

"Whatever, there are other folks of colour there, too." Mei tried to sound firm.

"Right—you, two other Asians, and a bunch of white queers. Sounds like hell."

Mei scowled.

"Come on Mei, I'm just playing with you. I don't care about sex positivity as much as I care about having positive sexual experiences. Lots of them. Stop being so sensitive. I'm gonna get Steven to take me back to his hotel. He's here on a business trip, which means room service!" Annette grinned again. "You wanna come? It'd been *fun!*"

Mei sighed. "Sorry about that. I'm gonna go. I'll see you tomorrow? Call me? I get worried."

"Suit yourself. I'll text you pictures," she winked.

Mei scowled again.

"And I'll call! Jesus."

"Thanks. I don't need pictures."

Mei turned to go and Annette followed her out, slapping her ass.

"Lighten up, honey."

Mei said good night to Steven and Annette, asked Nam, the bartender, if he would keep an eye on her friend, and started heading home. Annette said Mei had too many residual "man responsibility habits." Maybe this was correct, though still annoying, and Mei figured this particular habit was an okay one to keep.

Her walk home from the bar cuts past the bingo hall toward the park. Usually they blast classical music to keep kids from hanging out in front, smoking, but it's too late for that now. She points herself toward a bus stop. She doesn't need to walk through the park to get to the westbound buses, but it's a quick walk and she likes to pretend she's not surrounded by the city. The park is narrow, almost more of a boulevard, in the middle of two lanes of a busy street.

As she enters the park, she passes a group of men standing around in button-downs, dressed up for a night out, sharing a drink in the park before going off to their next destination. As she passes, one of them says, "Hey baby, come here."

She keeps walking, trying to think about food and not the man behind her. He calls out again, but she can't make out what he says. She keeps walking, a bit faster now. The air has cooled somewhat since the afternoon, the blistering humidity of the day having tempered. The residual summer heat makes the air taste deceptively neutral, coaxing her heart to beat deeper. Worried its beating will betray her, display her fear, she focusses on her speed through the park. On the proximity of the next street light. On how visible she is to passing cars.

She doesn't hear him walk up behind her, footfalls drowned out by heartbeats—just feels his shoulder touch hers as he appears next to her, his hand finding her ass.

"Baby," his voice mock pleads, "What are you walking away for?"

She feels his hand and instantly loses the heat of the summer night, her skin contracting, her heart making quick, erratic beats. She turns toward him, finding his face.

"Get off me!" she shouts. Her startled baritone betrays her.

The air catches the sound, slowing it, deepening it. His clean-cut face drops its grin. His shirt is well ironed, the sleeves rolled up to the elbows. She reads his panic, seeing it flame to anger, an inferno leaping from forest to field.

"What game are you playing? Faggot!" His words are wet with booze, quiet and forceful.

"Not quite," Mei manages, unthinking and terrified. She turns again and walks away quickly, hoping this protracted moment will end, fighting the urge to break into a run. The park's lights make patches on the path, the contrast making the dark areas even darker.

His friends have overheard their interaction and jeer at him. "Oh! You grabbed a dude's ass!" one yells, and laughter follows.

The man turns to them now. "I thought—fuck off!"

"Whatever you say," another responds, accompanied by more snickering. "Come on, let's leave these lovebirds to it."

Mei hears a chorus of thick laughter as they leave. Their departure brings a terrifying quiet to the park.

She is running now, only a few metres away from the street. The brick in her purse is heavy, comforting. She passes two men smoking on a bench, watching her run, unmoving. Her heart beats faster as she approaches the far edge of the narrow park, where the trees part and the light of the shops across the street shines into it. A border, an exit. She hears him coming, not a breath before she feels him. He strikes her from behind, sending her down to hands and knees. Rolling over, she swings her purse at him. One of the girls she knows from a drop-in had been attacked a few weeks ago. She had had a brick in her purse and was able to beat the guy and knock him out. Mei and Annette went looking for bricks the day they heard. Mei's purse hits her attacker's knee and she winds up for the next one at his head. He cries out and grabs her purse mid-swing, throwing it into the shadows. Grabbing her ankle with his other hand, he drags her back into the park, off the concrete path and onto the mulched bed of a garden. He curses her as she manages to hit him a few more times, but not enough to stop him.

༃

Hours later, Mei wakes to find her purse ripped open, her wallet emptied. Cards and change are scattered around her, all her different names littered in the

mulch. An explosion of identity. Gathering the change
and the IDs, she finds her shoes and tries, once more,
to walk to the bus.

Mei is cold. She doesn't know where to go
and automatically crosses the city on the bus, taking forty-five minutes to get to Connie's apartment.
Passengers get on and off. The irregular vibration
of the bus on broken pavement is comforting, and it
keeps Mei from imploding. Mei wishes for the autumn.
Not for the cooler air, but for the thicker clothes.
Something with a hood, a scarf.

A woman approaches the seat next to her and
stops, about to say something before catching herself.
She stares at Mei, with a hesitant half smile, her brow
tightened in the middle. Mei's upper lip curls at the
woman's pity and she looks directly into her eyes.
Mei's stare is a lock bolt, fixed and turning something
much larger and heavier than itself slowly and with
great force. The woman's pity turns to disgust.

"Well, you certainly had that coming!"

Mei spits blood on the floor, and the woman
walks toward the door of the bus.

ꙩ

Mei shows up at Connie's door. It is late, but she
knows Connie isn't sleeping. Even though she doesn't
stay out all night anymore, Connie can't fall asleep
any earlier than two in the morning. Usually it's later.
Connie had complained about it at the drop-in. Mei can
hear the radio; Connie is probably listening to one of
the dramas she convinced a worker at the community
centre to download for her. Connie had said she really

liked the sci-fi ones—stories focussed on different realities and non-human elements make her feel more at
home. Most of the time the racial bias of the authors is
so thinly veiled that she knows when they write about
aliens, they write about her. Genders they don't understand. Colours they can't place. That was Connie. That
was Mei. Whatever the program is tonight, she doesn't
hear Mei knocking.

Mei is knocking, though, with steady monot-
onous raps against the heavy door, the even rhythm
echoing in the hallway. The pounding of a clock. The
knock of the city. She knocks until one of Connie's
neighbours comes into the hall.

"Jesus! What are you doing? She isn't home!"
As Mei turns around, the neighbour sees her face. "Oh,
fuck. Are you okay? Connie! Connie, open up!" The
neighbour pounds on Connie's door with the panicked
regularity of a prey animal's heart, and Connie finally
answers.

"Aiyeoh. What happened to you?" She gently
touches Mei's cheek.

Mei looks at her face, locating the sound but
not the speaker.

"Sit down, Sai Mui."

Connie takes Mei's wrist and leads her to a
chair at the living room table. She walks into the kitch-
en, leaving Mei at the table. Mei hears a tap running.
The voices on the radio are overshadowed by the
exaggerated sound effects of the drama. Some story
about an alien pretending to be human. A creaking
door. Footfalls. The music of suspense. The sounds of

futuristic equipment. Whistles and bubbles. Science. The alien is trying to contact her home world, but her equipment is broken.

Connie pulls up a chair in front of Mei and places a bowl of hot water on the table. She pats a wet towel over Mei's face in silence, carefully softening the dried blood. On the radio, another alien, living in the same apartment building as the one with broken equipment, is also trying to contact home. Connie wrings the cloth out and starts wiping blood and gravel out of Mei's palms and knees. She shudders, and Mei notices her eyes become glassy as the cloth is dyed red.

"I used to do this for my son," Connie says quietly.

Mei did not know she had a son. Yet Connie had told Mei so many personal details. More stories about strangely shaped penises and how they felt than Mei could count, but Connie had never said a thing about her son.

"I cleaned gravel from his knees after a fight on the way home from school."

Mei, unresponsive, lets Connie clean her. Mei's knuckles are bruised, her knees and palms bloodied. Connie stands to clean Mei's forehead and notices blood coming out of her hairline.

"Aiya, your head, Sai Mui!" Connie whispers, and she walks back into the kitchen.

The second alien on the radio also can't contact his home world. The two of them have met, both pretending to be humans, in the elevator. Connie comes back with a bag of frozen peas, wrapped in a towel. She moves Mei's hand for her, and gets her to hold the peas against her head.

Connie sucks her teeth. "You are staying here tonight, Sai Mui. You are staying here tonight."

The aliens on the radio have fallen in love, each with the same unspoken secret. Each of them stranded. Mei's eyes focus on the brass legs of Connie's chair, the plastic coating peeling away, the shine tarnishing and chipping where it has been exposed.

Once Connie has removed the cloth, bowl, and peas, she sets Mei up on her sofa with a cup of chrysanthemum tea and goes back into the kitchen. Mei hears the clap of a knife on a cutting board, metal moving against ceramic. Connie emerges from the kitchen with the smells of ginger, green onion, and cooking fish. She takes her young friend's hand and says, "I help you. I am warming some congee."

The radio program is ending; another neighbour, a human, has discovered that there are aliens masquerading as humans in the apartment building and approaches the alien couple for help discovering the imposters. The music is full of suspense, lots of brass.

つ

In the morning, Mei wakes up on Connie's sofa to the sound of Connie speaking quietly in the doorway to her neighbour. Mei's phone rings, and Connie turns and smiles at Mei, stepping out into the hallway and closing the door.

Sandy is on the phone. He wants to let her know she left her sweater in Herbertsville after visiting last weekend. She thanks him. Her voice is quiet and thin. Sandy can tell something is wrong. He asks what's going on, if she is okay. She must sound worse than she thinks because his concern rises faster than she would have expected. Her eyes fill, but no tears come.

"Rough night," she says.

After a long pause, Sandy says he has a few more days off this week and can be down in the city tomorrow afternoon. She is angry at herself for being so transparent. She doesn't believe him, but lets the lie happen and invites him to stay with her. As Mei hangs up the phone, Connie comes back from the hallway. Her neighbour across the hall is wondering if Mei is okay. Connie, sitting beside her on the sofa, takes her hand and hugs her, casually and gently kissing her head. She opens a book and starts leafing through it. Mei leans into the sofa and lets herself relax. Connie and Sandy— what a pair of unlikely guardian angels, she thinks, as she drifts off.

ɔ

"Time to change the bandages, Sai Mui. Must keep it clean." Connie is gently rocking Mei's shoulder. Her smile is forced, but her eyes are reassuring to Mei; she can accept Connie's worry. It is sincere. In the bathroom, as Connie cleans Mei's wounds again, Mei's eyes rest on a calligraphy hanging on the wall. Connie had first pointed it out when Mei helped her move into this apartment.

———·———

"HEY, SAI MUI, you got big shoulders from be-fore hormones. You gonna help me move this week?" Connie grins at Mei, egging her on at the drop-in. Mei could swear Connie is deliberately offensive around her, especially when she's bored. There is no programming at the drop-in tonight, and dinner is late.

"Damn it, Connie!"

"Ha! She's just pissed cos she's still got a beer belly!" one of the other women at the drop-in yells out.

"You wanna rub it? It's lucky..." Connie returns. "So, you gonna help me move or what?"

ↄ

And now here she is, the only one helping Connie move, and Connie isn't really moving anything herself. Connie is moving to another apartment in the building she already lives in. Her new place is up a few floors.

"Closer to the penthouse," she winks, on the first load up. "If only my Ma could see me now. Finally successful." The apartment is half a block away from a bus station. It's an awkward area between neighbourhoods; everything is inconveniently spaced and the roads are too big to have much pedestrian traffic. There are a few apartment buildings in a row. They look as though they were built at the same time—each has a cracking grey stucco facade at the entrance and grey bricks up the walls. Above the door of Connie's building, it says *The Excelsior* in an embellished gold, curly font. The 'i' is dotted with a four-pointed star and the letters are shadowed with thin black lines. Connie has been there for more than a decade.

"Jesus, Connie." Mei is dragging a trunk down the hall to the elevator. "What do you have in here? A body?"

"Watch what you say! I do not have any more big luggage, and I don't want to have to get rid of you also," Connie whispers.

Mei lets go of the trunk and stares blankly at Connie, who stares back.

After an uncomfortable second, Connie laughs, shaking her head. "The look on your face! Ha! A body. Could you believe it? Me moving it house to house?"

"So what's in here?"

"Nothing to worry about," Connie replies, expressionless.

꩜

That evening, sitting on Connie's trunk, Mei eats noodles and soup while Connie unpacks. Mei notices a small jade statue of a horse amongst the things Connie is taking out of boxes. She picks it up and holds it.

"That came with me from Hong Kong. I'm a horse. Can't you tell?" Connie jokes.

"My Aunt Bernadette is, was, too," Mei says, not looking up. "When did you come here?"

Connie considers this for a moment before answering, "Hmm. Long time ago. 1970? Sai Mui, you seen this?" Connie passes Mei a small paint-ing with Chinese calligraphy on it. "You know that drop-in in the basement of that real estate building? I used to go there. One of the staff gave this to me as a housewarming. They helped me get this apartment. It is the five elements, but they are out of order! Aiyeoh. I love it. Put in the bathroom."

Mei looks at the painting, the five characters in a line. Sandy could read this; she isn't so good at it.

"I recognize fire and water..." Mei says, mostly to herself.

Connie sucks her teeth. "You know what, Sai Mui? You should get someone to teach you."

———.———

"WHAT THE HELL happened? Why were you alone? Why didn't you call me?" Sandy stands in the middle of Mei's apartment, yelling. Hazel is standing on the sofa wagging her tail, misinterpreting Sandy's high. He had arrived in the city the morning after he called. "You're so lucky it wasn't worse, you coulda got killed! You could have got—were you? Did he?"

Mei's eyes play tricks on her in the morning light. She is half listening to Sandy, tuning him out as she remembers the bus ride back to her apartment from Connie's earlier that day. Buildings had come into focus slowly as the bus drove down Main Street, and the moving vehicle had skewed her sense of time. The light through the bus windows seemed tangible; she had wanted to gather it and take it home. If she had done that, she could have shown Sandy, who is still very poorly processing what has happened. She pulls herself back into the apartment, into this moment with Sandy. She knew he would be upset when he saw her, but she has no energy to support him through this.

"You gotta stop, buddy. You're here to support me. Don't tell me I'm lucky. I know damn well what could have happened. And what did happen. Tell me what you're gonna cook me. Tell me what TV you've been watching. Don't be some weirdo dad cop or whatever." Her voice is quiet and firm. It hurts to talk, and it hurts to turn to look at him. But she would rather her mind focus on her pain than have it wander. Nothing feels right.

Sandy has raised his eyebrows and looks at her, his anger refocussing.

"I'm serious, Sandy. I don't have the energy for your bullshit right now." The effort tires her.

"Sorry. You should call the cops, though."

Mei stares at him. Slowly, painfully, she shakes her head. "And what do you actually think they are going to do to help this?" She draws out her words.

Sandy's face is a statue.

"You gotta figure out who you're mad at," she says. "Me? Or the guy that did this."

Sandy says he can stay with Mei for a few days, if she'd like. She finds it hard to accept his offer but loves the company he and Hazel bring to her one-bedroom apartment. She lets him sleep in her bed, and she takes the couch. With Hazel.

The first night Sandy stays, she cannot sleep. Mei sits with Hazel's head on her lap, running her hands through the dog's fur. She is awake, but the silence of her apartment and the darkness outside, broken by yellowed street lamps, gives the world around her a dreamlike quality. It is the time of night that feels endless. The time between.

By the third night of Sandy's visit, Mei is able to sleep. Exhaustion has caught up to her.

ↄ

Mei wakes up on the sofa to sounds in the kitchen, or the kitchen part of her apartment. It is probably morning. Sandy is standing over the stove. She smells soy milk heating. Sandy has been staying with her almost a week.

"Check out what I found downtown last night. Youtiao! I remember Aunt Jun making this. She made it better. I haven't had it in years."

"Amazing!"

She instantly regrets her enthusiasm. Her voice painfully echoes in her head. Sandy continues to get breakfast together in the kitchen. Mei looks out the window from the couch; the light of the street lamps has been replaced by the clear light of morning. Hazel is still beside her, sleeping.

"Hey Sandy?" Mei says.

He mumbles something in response, his back to her.

"What was it like to live with Nai Nai? Seriously," she asks.

He turns to her, chewing a piece of youtiao and wiping the oil from the fried dough on his pant leg.

"It was great. Seriously," he says.

"Actually? She was angry all the time! Like all the time. She hated your mother."

"She didn't hate Ma, and you weren't there all the time. She was hard on Ma for sure, but Aunt Jun was the eldest, I think she was way harder on her. Nai Nai was way cooler than you could know."

"What is that supposed to mean? Was she a smuggler?" Mei sits up quickly, excited at the possibility, then winces.

"She didn't go anywhere. What would she smuggle?" Sandy scoffs, dipping a length of youtiao in the pot of soy milk heating on the stove and biting off the now soggy tip.

"I mean, before. Before she came to Canada. When she was in China. Once, she told me she knew how to sail a boat. A tiny fast one." Mei's eyes narrow, imagining her Nai Nai moving at great speeds through the salty sea air.

"Oh yeah! I don't know if she smuggled any-thing. Why do you want her to be a smuggler?" he says between bites.

"I don't know, I guess I just don't know any-thing about them. Mom, Aunt Bernadette, Nai Nai. So I make it up. Give me some of that."

Out the window, there are no clouds. Mei gives up on finding out more about Nai Nai. They should probably take Hazel out to the park. Into the Canadian postcard of a day outside. It is not a picture she wants to enter; she prefers to remain out of focus and hidden.

"I can tell you one thing," Sandy offers, breaking Mei's daydream and instantly regaining her full attention. "She was always talking to dead rela-tives. She used to say that Canadians treated their dead like they treated their elderly. They send them to a graveyard or a nursing home and forget about them." He takes another bite of youtiao. "She lived with the dead." Sandy walks across the room and hands her a bowl of soy milk.

"Canadians. She just meant white people, but she always said Canadians," Mei mutters, taking the bowl. "Thanks."

"She called it like she saw it," Sandy says, hand-ing her a plate of youtiao before coming to sit beside her with a bowl of soy milk of his own.

Mei notices a flash of white on the back of his hand, a bandage. His knuckles are wrapped and blood is seeping through. She hadn't noticed it when he was across the room at the stove.

"Where'd you go last night?" she asks, staring at his hand.

Sandy shrugs. "Me? I just went out for a walk. Downtown. How'd you sleep?"

"Pretty good. Weird dream I can't remember. Seriously, what happened to your hand?" Mei leans over to him. "You get in a fight or something?" She points at his hand with a youtiao, squinting.

He pulls it away, reaching for his own piece.

"Nah, I just slipped walking Hazel this morning and hit my hand. I wasn't paying attention walking up some stairs. Texting. You know."

Mei knows Sandy is lying.

"Fine, don't tell me," she scowls.

Sandy pretends to be hurt.

She looks at him for moment, realizing how thankful she is for his company, and says, "Thanks for breakfast."

He reaches out with his bandaged hand and squeezes her knee.

They eat in silence, breathing in each other's presence, eating one of the few meals they remember Nai Nai cooking. China is a myth to them. Something they only see evidence of in their skin, their eyes. Their family. Each other. They have never been. They still assume that Jun had gone back years ago, but she left no way of contacting her. Jun did not take Mei to

Chinatown when they went to the capital, an hour away from Dundurn, and she only started to celebrate Chinese New Year after Nai Nai berated her for raising a white boy. China is stories from Nai Nai, a mix of exaggeration and truth, information that is decades out of date. Bernadette bought Mei and Sandy some Mandarin cartoons one Christmas, which were strange and unfamiliar to them. Sandy loved them and quickly convinced Mei to love them as well.

"Who at your school gets to watch shows like this? Anyone? This is for *us*," Sandy had said to Mei. He was right, no one at her school knew any of the shows she watched with Sandy. As adults, they eat at Chinese restaurants, trying to remember what Nai Nai cooked in the restaurant before Bernadette convinced her to sell it when she got sick. They romanticize the memory of the dishes so much they are never sure they have ordered the correct ones. The tastes are never exactly as they remember them. They hold a sense of entitlement to an experience they have never had.

Sandy breaks the silence of their meal and turns to Mei, saying, "I'm going to have to go back to Herbertsville tonight. They won't give me any more time off. I'm surprised I got to stay this long. I took your library card and got some of those weird short films you like. The colourful ones that look like they were made by hippies with a healthy budget."

Mei sits up. "They were made by hippies with a healthy budget.

"You would have been proud of me, Sandy. When that guy came at me. I got him good before he knocked me out. Right in the knee like you used to say I should. I bet he's got a good limp on this week," she grins, then winces. "It hurts to smile."

"Yeah, you told me already. But you said you got him in the shoulder." Sandy stops stirring the last of his milk with a heel of youtiao. His hand shakes.

Mei stiffly gets up and walks across the room to turn on the kettle. "Nope. Right in the knee. It's the weakest joint. That's why you gotta aim for it. I learned that in—"

"You said you got him in the shoulder!" Sandy points the tiny piece of fried bread at her, staring, his eyebrows angled, frustrated. An expression without nuance.

"What is with you?" Mei stares back at him, scowling. "Calm down. What difference does it make?"

Sandy's eyes widen. "It makes a huge difference," he says softly, then pauses. "Sorry I'm just ... I just have to go to the bathroom." He stands, rubbing the back of his head with his bandaged hand.

"Whatever you say. You're such a weirdo."

Sandy smiles, absently walking into the bathroom. Mei hears the unoiled fan turn on, moving out of habit, then the toilet seat lift, then Sandy vomiting.

ɔ

When Nai Nai was dying, Sandy and Mei travelled through the dark end of a spring night, away from the sunrise, away from Herbertsville to the larger town to the west. To the closest hospital. Mei remembers this as a trip to another world. A kingdom of bridges connecting the dead and the living.

The hospital was a maze. Mei had learned the difference between a maze and a labyrinth from a kid at school. Mazes had dead ends and tricks. Labyrinths had one way in, but no way out. Unless you turned around and walked back out the way you came. She was younger, much younger. Still a little boy, six or seven. She was with Sandy and Bernadette walking to meet her mother, who had been there all night. The corridors were full of grey machines with yellow screens and people in loose clothing running with clipboards. Cords and wires. Tubes. Labyrinths inside a maze.

After turning and winding through the hospital, through red sections and blue sections, following coloured tape lines on the floor, they turned toward a room where Mei's mother was sitting on the edge of a bed that held Nai Nai. She got up when she saw them approaching. She looked at Mei and Sandy, offering them a faint smile, then at Bernadette, and nodded subtly.

"Go see your Nai Nai," Bernadette directed Sandy. "She is close now and you must see her. Take Xiao Er. She will want to see him too."

Sandy took Mei by the hand and they walked into the hospital room. Mei had been staying with Bernadette and Sandy in Herbertsville, the town beside this other world. Jun had called while Bernadette was getting breakfast for Sandy and Mei.

"Wéi? Ah. Jun. Hǎo. Okay. Wǒ men lái le." Bernadette had turned to Sandy and Mei blankly, which signalled Sandy to find Mei's coat and boots. They had piled into Bernadette's beige Topaz and driven the twenty minutes to the hospital in rising spring sun through the sleeping fields of Herbertsville. Mei took in the lights of the larger town that served most of the towns in the area. When they had arrived the hospital was dimly lit but full of activity. Nurses moved quickly, but didn't rush, from room to room. People waited by vending machines and water fountains. Drinking midnight coffees.

Nai Nai's room smelled like sleep and disinfectant. She moved slowly, waking up or falling asleep, eyes registering the children.

"Xiǎo hái. Lái. Come. You are good for your mothers? Ah?" Nai Nai asked, rising as she pushed the remote controls on the bed. Her voice was quiet but happy. She was calm, her breath slow and laboured.

"Shì!" Sandy and Mei said in unison, nodding.

"Ha ha. Hǎo. Good."

Mei fidgeted, uncomfortable with the space, the arrangement.

"Xiao Er," Nai Nai said to Mei, pointing at the drawer beside her bed. "Kāi le."

Mei opened it to find a bag of hard candies. This was the earliest in the morning anyone had ever allowed her to have candy.

"Eat it," Nai Nai said, smiling and rubbing Mei's head. "Gěi tā."

Mei took a candy and handed the bag to Sandy.

"Sandy. You must watch Xiao Er. His strong not the same as your strong. You are the oldest," said Nai Nai, taking Sandy's hand and squeezing it gently.

He nodded, silent, while Mei slowly began to

understand that something important was happening. Nai Nai usually told Sandy he was not doing a good enough job. Sandy was wearing a serious expression Mei did not recognize. He looked almost angry.

"Xiǎo hái, do not look so worry. I keep eyes on you. Be good to—" Nai Nai coughed, grabbing Mei's hand and startling her. Nai Nai tried to keep the coughing under control but it quickly became a fit, her mouth opening, lower lip extended, her head tilting back. It looked as if something was rising from her chest. Alarms on the machines started to peal, unearthly bells calling in the nurses. Someone picked up Mei and brought the two children out of the room.

There was a funeral in the city the following week. Bernadette and Sandy came to stay with Mei and her mother in the days leading up to the service. A few days before the funeral, a boy down the street from Jun's house made fun of Mei's name—"Shaw Ear! Straw Ear!"—and pushed her down while she and Sandy were outside. Sandy hit the boy and a fight started. He paid his respects to Nai Nai with a black eye, while his mother, puffy eyed, sucked her teeth and quietly shook her head.

She is looking at the shoreline under her feet. Water gathers at her ankles, icy in the mid-morning, as she sits on the sand. Raising her head and pushing the wet dark hair off of her face, she stares at the shoreline drawing out in the distance, splitting the lake and peninsula into separate parts, or maybe joining them together. She imagines sketching the pattern for a quilted patch of this view, placing a black dot at the farthest point she can distinguish and tracing backward to the outside of her field of view. The water at this time of day is the cobalt blue of the glass bottles Bernadette had collected. In a few hours the sun will have moved, splitting the lake into brown, turquoise and ultramarine. The sand is nearly white against the rich green of cedar trees spreading shallow roots in the loose soil.

She imagines the patch on the quilt and returns to her feet.

A VELVET LINING

SANDY KNOWS THE narrow park Mei was attacked in. He knows the bingo hall blasting classical music. He has walked through it with college friends, drunk men yelling and spilling out into the warm late summer night. The sunlight has been replaced by the lights of the city. Sandy has left Mei asleep on the couch, but Hazel will keep an eye on her. She can be terrifying when she is feeling protective. This makes him feel better about leaving Mei alone while he is out in the street, hunting.

It is early enough that the bars haven't let out. The street lights cut through the grass, illuminating and concealing simultaneously. Entering the park, he walks along the concrete path. The street lights do not catch much of the park. Most of it is lined by a small fence that stops people from running into traffic. Or from traffic running into the park. The park is as he remembers it. He notices two silhouettes on a bench, two men drinking. He takes a deep breath and approaches them.

"Hey, you guys. You hang out here much?"

"Maybe," the older one replies. "You sure don't."

"It's not always the best place to meet strangers," comes a warning from the younger one.

"Well, you guys seem pretty comfortable. So I figure you're here a lot. I'm looking for someone."

"That's sweet," says the older one. "Lost your boyfriend?"

"Something like that. You see a guy beat up a girl here last week?"

"Whoa. Right to the chase, eh? Nah. We didn't see anything."

"Yeah, we left when we saw—" The younger man stops as the older one hits his chest.

"What's with him?" Sandy asks, pulling out a flask. He takes a long, slow swig. "Sounds like you might be able to help me out. That girl was my cousin."

Sandy sits with the two men on the bench for hours, sharing his liquor. He discovers that one of the men grew up one town east of Herbertsville. They know some of the same people. The other one is from out west. The bottle is getting low when the man from east of Herbertsville leans over and tells Sandy he might like to talk to the guy coming down the path toward them. Sandy's companions get up and quietly walk out of the park.

"Hey there."

The man walking toward him looks up. "What do you want?"

It looks like Mei dislocated his shoulder and broke a few of his fingers before he knocked her out.

"You look like you're in rough shape. You want a drink?" Sandy asks.

The man's expression relaxes.

Sandy hands him the flask. "Finish it."

"Uh ... thanks?" The man shrugs and takes the flask.

They watch each other carefully.

"Of course," says Sandy. "It's no problem. I think we might have a friend in common."

"Oh yeah?"

ɔ

An hour later, walking back to Mei's apartment, Sandy's eyes wander from the cracked sidewalk littered with black and grey gum spots, past the neon signs of the buildings around him and up to the few brilliant stars whose light manages to penetrate the glow of the city. His hand aches. He thinks of his mother, wondering what she would think of the things he has done.

BERNADETTE IS DYING. Refusing to go to the hospital, she sits with Sandy in their kitchen at the small wooden table. It will take Sandy more than a month to realize that he is terrified of being left alone, and that is why he asks again and again about illnesses in the family. He heard a radio program about hereditary diseases on the way to work.

"We needed help. Diane didn't want to carry a baby, and didn't really want to be a mother. It was my idea. My desire. I wanted a baby and our friend Donnie Lau had the missing factors."

Sandy and Bernadette are waiting for the kettle to boil. The overhead light is milk white and dim like a full moon, only full of dead bugs.

"Missing factors? Like appropriate humidity or enough nitrogen? You make it sound like some kind of science experiment."

Bernadette has always been excited about science; in another life, she would have been a quirky professor or a fun middle school science teacher. She liked to set up small experiments for Sandy when he was a child or take him for walks in the woodlot near their house, pointing out plants, bugs, and mushrooms. He had loved learning about acids and bases by making a volcano with vinegar and baking soda, but learning about melting points by salting ice cubes was actually as engaging as it sounded and he lost interest. And apparently, the at-home science experiments had been an aspect of every element of his childhood.

"Well ... it kind of was."

Hearing this, Sandy shakes his head, getting up and impatiently moving the kettle on the burner, as if it must be adjusted to boil. There are two cups and a teapot on the counter, waiting. He has already heard what comes next and hasn't been interested in the details since he was a small child. At least now he does not worry about Nai Nai's reaction to such questions. He can predict the words as Bernadette says them:

"It involved the three of us hanging out with a glass jar, a syringe with the needle off and ... you don't want to know all this. Besides, didn't I teach you anything? Science is—"

He cuts her off, "—all around us, yeah yeah. I'm not six. I've had lots of sex and I know—"

"Sandy! Lots? Were you safe?"

"Bernadette! Aiya! Stop changing the subject." He is suddenly angry, using her first name. He watches her face shift, a river eddy suddenly smooth as glass with faint motion along the edges, currents moving swiftly below. He is instantly calm again. "I want to know about any possible medical conditions; I want to know what to watch out for in myself. With you so sick, Aunt Jun's diabetes and, well, and Nai Nai. Dying of—"

"Sandy, I am your mother. Diane, well ... Diane too."

"I know, Ma. I'm sorry I yelled. But Diane?" His shoulders tense and bile rises in his throat. "You can't be serious. Where is she?" He puts the cups on the table and sits down with the pot.

Bernadette looks thoughtfully at her cup. Her body is smaller each day. Her skin is greying. But her mind is sharp like the tip of a flame, definite and ethereal. He pours her tea and she gently taps the table beside it. The pause tells Sandy everything he does not want to know about the effect of Diane's absence.

"I can't answer that, because I don't know either. But what I do know is that I love her—loved her. She made me happy, Sandy. Don't scoff. It's true. She understood me, so well. She just never understood herself. Every time she came back I believed it would be different. And you know, every time it was a little different. But never different enough. She couldn't handle Nai Nai's disapproval, and she couldn't understand that I needed to take care of my mother. She didn't know what she wanted. She left and it became clear I was doing this mostly on my own. Nai Nai and I helped each other. Even if she hated who I am." She looks at the cup of tea in her hand.

Sandy, following her eyes, stares at the cup as well. She turns the cup slowly, and Sandy knows she is watching the liquid remain parallel to the ground, no matter how she moves it.

"Mei always liked the science experiments," she says absently, changing the subject. As though her emotions are catching their breath. "Anyway, after all of that, I lost touch with Donnie. It was never part of the agreement that he stay on and help raise you. I just needed, well. You know what I needed. I heard he moved to Vancouver. Met a nice man, liked the winters, and stayed. Can't say I blame him." She looks up and grins, her dark hair framing her thin face. She is under two sweaters and a quilt. "I don't know what illnesses he had."

"Ma. I'm *sorry.* I know all this. I just want to know. You know? Stuff like heart disease, or maybe cancer or I don't know, anything." His fingers rattle on the table at his own persistence; he can't give up. But he knows he may not be able to ask again and that Mei has even less of an idea about their family.

"People question too much about me, Sandy. I don't need them asking around if you are my son."

"Ma. We were the only Asians in Herbertsville when I was born. Even if we were as unrelated as Amy Tan and Margaret Cho, they would have thought I was your son."

"Ha. Margaret Cho. Now there is funny lady." Her laugh is abrupt but sincere. "Is the stove off?"

"Yes."

"They said Nai Nai had heart disease and high cholesterol. Jun has diabetes. And then there's me. That's what I can tell you about illness. Nai Nai didn't take medical records with her when she left." Bernadette looks up at Sandy, who cannot make eye contact with her. He has heard little about how and why Nai Nai left China, but he knows enough to not to judge whatever was or wasn't done to get out. Of course they don't know.

"You are frightened, Sandy. I know. But I am not going to hospital. I was a nurse there for almost thirty years. All of the people I trusted are dead or retired and all of the new nurses are younger than Mei.

Like hell I'm going to let them take care of me; they should be taking care of their own grandmothers. Now drink your tea and tell me about all this sex you've been having."

T HE AIR IS cold but he welcomes it. It is grounding and relieving to feel the ephemeral character of body heat. In the moment between chopping the last of the wood and the somatic realization of winter, he is a new planet, a molten core spinning furiously, volcano plumes billowing out of his breath. If not for the solidity of the ground below him, he would believe that he orbited the forest instead of walked in it. Bernadette has been dead for two weeks. Mei has just headed back to the city after visiting for a few days following the funeral. Hazel is sitting on a pile of pine boughs while he splits logs in the woodlot.

Walking back to the house, he sees Diane's truck in the drive. He hasn't seen her in more than a year. Not while Bernadette was sick, not at the funeral. He left messages on her phone, and he knew his mother had left more. Hazel notices her and runs ahead, barking.

"Hey Sandy!" Diane calls. "I was just stopping by to get some things." She gives a forced, quick smile as he approaches.

"What things? Did you go in the house?" He feels his blood heating his face.

Ultimately, Bernadette had not wanted to see Diane before she died. Her expectation that Diane would break a promise to visit was no longer something Bernadette would tolerate. The absence of a final interaction was a painful one, for Sandy and for Bernadette.

"Look, I know you're angry—" Diane starts.

"What did you take? Those are her things!" he fires back at her.

Diane's face hardens. "Our things. She was my partner. We are a family, Sandy."

"No. We weren't. Nothing here is yours. You gave up that right when you couldn't take care of her. If I had been old enough to tell her not to take you back after bailing on us when I was a baby, I would have. But you slipped back in. Just like you're trying to slip back now." His cheeks, already flushed from chopping wood, are now red with anger.

"Sandy ... You just—you don't know what you're talking about. It's not as simple as that," Diane says, nearly pleading. Her defence is unenthusiastic, as if she does not entirely believe it herself.

"I'll tell you what I know, Diane. She was so happy to see you when you came back the last time. I remember that. Clear as I see you now. So completely happy. Of course I wanted you around, but you kept slipping out. You couldn't handle it. And then she got sick, and you were gone. Again. Simple as that."

Hazel watches them intently, reading their interaction, determining if this is play or combat.

"I couldn't be here for that. I wasn't what she needed. But I am still your family. We planned it together. We—" Diane says, making sheepish eye contact, her voice quieter now.

"Plans don't mean a thing. She loved you, Diane! She wanted you around and you couldn't handle it, so you bailed. And now she's dead. And you're stealing her things. Get out. Give me your key and get the fuck out of here." He does not often curse. The word hits Diane heavily. Sandy's mouth is vehement, his gaze steady. He doesn't even care what she has taken. He wants to never see her on the property again.

"I just took the tapes," she admits, uncoiling the key from her key ring. Her back is straighter, her voice louder. She breaks eye contact. Sandy's firm rejection has given her confidence.

This only incenses Sandy further. "Fine, Diane. I don't need recordings of your voice pleading empty apologies to my dying mother. It's not something I look forward to listening to when I'm old. I tried to get her to erase them, but she wouldn't. She just boxed them and labelled them like everything else." He holds his hand out, waiting impatiently for the key.

She puts it in his hand.

"You see this, Diane? The teeth on this key, they're still sharp. You didn't cut a new one, did you?"

Diane shakes her head.

"Because Ma never changed the lock. Not once. This key is older than I am and the teeth aren't even worn down. That's how much you were here."

Diane is silent. She looks at Sandy. "I hate that you're so angry.

"Good thing you're not my mother. Otherwise, your opinion might matter."

Diane retreats, slamming the door to her truck but not driving off. Protected by the door, she stares down the road for a moment before turning back to Sandy. "I didn't just come here for the tapes, Sandy.

I came here to tell you that you are the person I most admire."

Sandy, startled by the sudden vulnerability, says nothing and then scoffs.

"I'm serious, Sandy. Of all the things you could have learned from me taking off, from me coming back and being in and out of your life, you learned such fierce devotion to the people you love. I admire it." She is wringing the steering wheel with her hands.

Sandy walks up to the truck. "I didn't learn that from you. Maybe you had a hand it, but just a hand. I learned that because it was just her and me. Because after Aunt Jun was gone, Mei was left alone too. Because it was just me at school, at work. Because my mother was an excellent mother. You were never one of us, never one of the family. You might have wanted to be, but I knew you weren't all along. You never hurt me because you couldn't. But you hurt her."

"I know I did, Sandy."

"You don't even know what that means! Listen to you, trying to take credit for how I turned out. You want to know what you taught me? The inevitability of betrayal. Once the traitor is out of the house, make sure she stays out. That is your legacy. I asked you to leave. You best do that. Come, Hazel."

Sandy walks away from the truck, and Hazel follows.

ɔ

The summer Sandy met Diane was dry. Incredibly dry. Sandy was almost seventeen, and he had a job working for a landscape construction company. They were installing a storm water management pond, a new requirement from the province. The ponds were meant to help control flooding during heavy rains and melts. They were trying to plant the pond that had been dug. The soil was hard packed, dry and cracking. He had an easier time fitting his shovel between the cracks in the clay than digging new holes for the plants in what was, according to the diagrams, supposed to be the bank of the small marshy pond they were putting in. It was strange to Sandy: Installing a pond, diagrams of wetlands. The calculation of control. The appropriation of the innate techniques of the land. The pond was an unnatural perfect square with slopes angled at a perfect forty-five degrees that ran for thirty perfect feet from top to bottom.

He was planting the wetland plants at the bottom of the slope, but the ground was solid and unyielding. These plants had come from a greenhouse where they had lived in warm shallow water, and they had been brought to this rigid place. The heat was baking, pulling the moisture out of Sandy and all the plants. When he finally would wrestle the plants into the hard ground, their stems were often broken, and if they weren't broken, the geese, lining the top of the sloping banks of the pond, were ready to waddle down and eat them, the only fresh, green, moist thing in the area. Sandy hated that they ate everything and that he would just have to replant the next day, but he was being paid by the hour and, if he were a goose, he would have been doing exactly the same thing.

Sandy's sweat soaked through his shirt and

evaporated, moving on from the heat, leaving him, shovel in hand, to deal with it. The land had worked perfectly well, managing its own storm water, before someone had come along and paved everything, he thought. It felt cruel, a landscape brutalized but surviving, thriving in some parts but left with the damage, and these new plants selected for a job that was impossible to do but forced here because they really had no other choice. Perhaps he was overthinking the situation. But he had been coming to this site every day for a week, doing the same thing every day. And every day, the same gaggle of geese lined the top of the pond, watching from the ridge, patiently waiting for the workers to leave.

This continued for a week, until in a fit, the engineer who had made the diagrams came to the site and demanded why the plants weren't in the pond. Sandy's foreman told the engineer about the drought and the geese. He explained that it wouldn't work and that he couldn't keep replacing the plants. The engineer said he would find another contractor if this crew "wasn't up for it." That day his boss told him not to bother to come back to the transformer station job site.

ↄ

He woke up as the sun was rising. He was standing in the kitchen, preparing to leave for his first day at a new job site—culvert work on a rail line. The red light of the sun swelled through the windows of the house. He heard a bedroom door open, and a woman walked into the kitchen. She had short, greying hair. She held a button-down shirt in her hands and was wearing a tank top and shorts. They stared at each other for a long time.

"Sandy?" the woman asked.

"Uh. Yes? Who are you?" Sandy was holding a cup of coffee.

"Are you old enough to drink that?" she asked.

"Yes. Who are you?" Sandy asked again, putting the coffee cup down on the counter.

"Sorry, it's just that—you're so big. I'm Diane." She held out her hand in introduction.

Sandy had heard about Diane. His mother had shown him pictures of her from when she was much younger. Diane was supposed to be his mother. She was also meant to raise him. Sandy knew her only as the woman his mother loved, the woman his mother still spoke highly of despite her absence of more than a decade. He could tell his mother loved her, waited for her. He could tell this from the distance in his mother's eyes when she spoke about Diane, when she spoke about how she came to have a son. Every telling of the story came with a half-hearted smile, a failed attempt to convince Sandy it was a happy story. Sandy knew this love made his mother vulnerable. It put her in danger, and this dangerous woman had returned. He did not take her hand.

"What are you doing here?" Sandy demanded.

Diane did not answer. She blinked several times, quickly, before widening her eyes, an instant of a frown before an awkward laugh.

"Is there more coffee?" she asked, but did not receive an answer.

Diane stayed for a week. Bernadette was beaming. Sandy had never seen her that happy. Each morning he spent the half-hour walk along the tracks to the new job site wondering if his mother was right to be happy. Just as he was beginning to trust his mother's love for Diane, he came home from work to find her, puffy eyed and silent, sitting in the kitchen. Her pain darkened the room on the bright late summer afternoon. He walked past her, gently touching her shoulder, and put the kettle on.

"Hē bù hē chá? Do you want some tea?" he asked, not expecting an answer. "You want dumplings for dinner? I froze some from the weekend." He sat down as Bernadette gave him an empty smile and took his calloused hand across the table.

꙾

Sandy was the only guy that wasn't white on his crew. At this job site, they needed to walk in from the road a half kilometre to the culvert they were fixing. It was a frustrating walk in; they carried all the tools in buckets, stumbling over the awkwardly spaced rail ties. On the walk out, they were tired, covered in swamp water and bug bites. One day, a guy on the crew asked what Sandy's grandmother would think of him back working on the railroad. The sun wasn't fully risen and it was already baking hot. Sandy put down the tools he was carrying and asked him to repeat what he had just said. The other worker put down his bucket of tools and turned around into Sandy's right fist.

Sandy's foreman said he had broken the guy's nose, but that the worker wouldn't press charges.

"Well, can I press charges for him being a racist?" Sandy asked.

"He was just joking around, Sandy. Lighten up."

"If I get any lighter, I'll start making racist jokes too. I'm going home now."

ɔ

Sandy later got certified as a substation maintenance technician and found himself working back at the transformer station. It was a union job, with a special clause in the collective agreement about racism, and there was dental coverage. On his first call to the station, years after he'd first worked on it, the plants still weren't in the ground around the bank of the storm water management pond, but the geese were there.

ɔ

Sandy did not see Diane until the next year, when she returned to repeat the pattern. Repetitions are never identical; the passage of time makes every interaction unique. Each of the three times Diane appeared again, Sandy refused to speak with her or Bernadette. He felt unable to stop the coming storm.

——————•——————

AFTER DIANE HAS faded into a bitter memory, scarred over and no longer tender, Sandy returns home to find his mother calling her on the phone.

"Diane, I need to see you. It's important. I—" She turns to see Sandy standing in the doorway to the kitchen, his mouth open, forehead creased. "I have to go. Call me back." Bernadette hangs up the phone. "You're back earlier than I expected."

"Why were you calling her?" Sandy asks, his voice quiet, more confused than angry.

Bernadette does not answer him. That was the first time. Over the coming months Sandy overhears other phone messages to Diane. They are heartbreaking.

She never answers his demands for explanation. "This is not something you would understand," she rebuts, flatly.

As he comes to understand that she is ill, and she comes to admit it, her motives become clearer. She knows she is dying. She leaves a final message on Diane's phone, explaining the urgency. Asking her to come. Sandy is with her when she calls; he cannot protest the desire to see her lover again. Diane does not return her call. In the weeks before her death, Bernadette stops waiting for Diane, even when she starts calling her back, every day, to offer excuses and apologies but never visiting. Bernadette will not answer the phone, but lets the answering machine take the calls. Bernadette labels a box *Diane* and throws the tapes in as they are filled.

"GLASS WAS EVERYWHERE. On the bed. All over the carpet. All over the bookshelf. In your hair." Bernadette touches his black hair, too short now for much of anything to be caught in it. Bernadette is in and out of sleep. Sandy is sitting in her room with her, leaning out of his chair to hear her speak from her bed in the late summer night. She recalls a storm. She recalls being a young mother of a young child. This is a story Sandy has not heard before. Bernadette is narrating, idly stroking Sandy's head. He is not sure if she is describing a dream or a memory.

He hears the story as if it is a scene unfolding outside of his mother's bedroom window. He can see her words play out in the new moon darkness. First, the sound of the storm. He sees himself, a young boy, asleep, sick in early autumn and Bernadette sitting alone in the kitchen. She is watching the storm, embroidering a swallow onto a quilt, her hands moving slowly. Her own mother sleeps in her room, the white noise of the storm holding her in a dream. Bernadette is practicing a blanket stitch, the needle returning to the loop it just made, revisiting the idea before moving on to the next. A co-worker at the hospital has taught her to count the seconds as "steamboats" between lightning flashes and thunder claps to measure how near they are to the storm.

She is quietly counting "two steamboat, three steamboat." She hears a noise the colour of fireworks. So startling the sound, it is not buried in the thunder of the storm outside. She turns to face the noise. She was expecting thunder, counting seconds after a lightning flash, watching the sky balance itself. Charge for charge. Two-and-a-half seconds before she expected a boom, she got a crash. The sound of a window crashing into the house, tremendous.

Bernadette exhales, then continues to narrate the hours leading up to the incident.

"It was terrifying. Nothing was working fast enough to break the fever and you were hallucinating. Your brain beginning to cook in your blood. The acetaminophen was taking too long. I suddenly stopped trusting anything made to stop a fever. The sky took the lightning, I thought it might take your fever. I wanted to run with you into the storm, cool you down. But I was worried it would make you sicker."

A pause, time enough for Sandy to consider her worry. The young Bernadette is putting down her sewing and running into Sandy's room.

"I sat with you until you fell asleep," the monologue continues. "I went back out to the kitchen to count the seconds between the light and the sound, and to sew, hoping the medication would drop the fever, not wanting Nai Nai to know how serious it had become. She would know what a poor mother I was. Then I heard the crash."

Sandy feels her speed as she flies to his bedroom.

"To you, my sleeping son. The lightning exposed the room with each bolt."

Sandy can picture the tableau of himself surrounded by glass, and beside him on the bed, whatever has hurled through the window, its neck broken. Some kind of bird—a goose.

"I saw the goose. It was enormous next to your little body. How high in the air would it have to be to look like the shallow silhouettes I had been seeing as the geese flew south for the winter? This one was going to stay in the north. How far from the ground, far from the window, and far from you had this bird come?"

The younger Bernadette's voice rises with concern, stirring the younger Sandy, who rolls over to put his arm around the body of the bird.

In the bedroom now, Bernadette struggles to sit up in bed. She looks at Sandy, more lucid, and continues her story.

"I was so worried about you, my boy, that I did not see Nai Nai standing beside your bed. She was furious with me, like I knew she would be. She told me your fever was gone and that I was wrong not to tell her—" Bernadette winces, pain waking her further, "—not to tell her how sick you were." She looks away from Sandy. "Then she said the strangest thing; you know how she was. She looked at me and said, 'If you told me he is this sick, I could fix it and he would not have this debt to carry,' and then she walked out of the room. Leaving me to clean up the glass and deal with the bird."

"Why didn't you tell me that before?" Sandy asks, unsure where to place this story, how seriously to consider Nai Nai's statement.

"I don't know, it was just so—so strange, Sandy. The window, the idea of you having a 'debt' or something."

His eyes flash, unimpressed with the answer.

Sighing, Bernadette concedes, "I should have told you sooner. I guess I just don't like to think about that period too much. I was alone. Diane was gone. She had said she'd parent you with me: 'We're going to live the dream, lesbian moms in the country.' Wouldn't that have been something? But she took off just before you were born. I gave birth to you alone in the hospital. Nai Nai and Aunt Jun came, but they brought their disapproval. Some of the girls from the hospital stopped by, but I was so lonely. I went to school to be a nurse. Got a job at the hospital. Everyone wanted to know about your 'father.' And I was the only Asian in town except for Nai Nai. Boy, was everyone confused when you turned out to be full blooded. Everyone just assumed some local boy had got me pregnant. Even now, I think Mrs. Daniels is suspicious of how a Chinaman snuck into Herbertsville and knocked me up without her noticing. Wouldn't she have been shocked to see us, Diane with a turkey baster, me on the bed, and Donnie Lau with a jar full of his sperm!" She laughs, but the laughter brings on a cough she cannot control.

ɔ

In a week, Bernadette is dead, a series of five small strokes in her sleep as Sandy sleeps beside her on a cot in her room.

DIANE SITS ON the stairs in her quiet, empty house. She has only moved one step all afternoon. She has missed her chance. Bernie is dead. She'd asked Diane to come see her, but Diane couldn't and Bernie had stopped trying. But then, when Diane had changed her mind and pleaded to come over, message after message, Bernie had finally caved.

"Come see me," she had said, and suddenly Diane couldn't. She was overcome with guilt, pickling in it. Guilt for not being there. Guilt for leaving. For harassing her. Going to see her, so close to death, would have only driven home the irreparable effect of her actions. Bernie had Sandy; she wasn't alone. But Diane, without her broken relationship with Bernie, she doesn't have a thing. Just a job at a quarry and an empty house. Everything about the house is amplified. The musty smell of the carpet, the rough hum of the fridge fighting to stay cold. The funeral is in a few days. She won't go—no one expects her to. She moves another step, and looks out the open front door. The skeletal trees look like cracks in the horizon, as if the sky had collided with the field, expecting to be caught by the gentle foliage of a forest.

ᴐ

Diane and Bernie were sitting in the kitchen. Diane still couldn't believe everything had worked with

Lau. But it had, and Bernie's belly rose like a mountain of proof. It was an outlandish plan, but Bernie wanted to have a baby. Diane wanted to be with Bernie, wanted to be committed to her, and having a baby seemed like a great idea. Now, with the pregnancy moving along and Diane hanging around the house more, it was feeling increasingly real. Jun had gone to live with her boyfriend and rarely came by. She still worked in the restaurant with their mother, but only Bernie and her mother lived at the house. Soon Diane would join them.

Bernie's mother had noticed the pregnancy early on, well before Bernie had planned to tell her. Bernie was convinced that a baby, something she and her mother had wanted in the family, would soften the blow of Bernie coming out. But the opposite turned out to be true. As far as her mother was concerned, the baby had no father, and her relationship with Diane was disgusting. Initially, she had been quietly opposed to the baby and the relationship, but as Bernie became more visibly pregnant and customers in the restaurant noticed, Bernie's mother became more openly hostile.

In recent weeks, Bernie's mother regularly criticized her, refused her help with anything, and openly insulted her. It was killing Diane to see it.

"Why don't you say something, or leave? Come stay with me at my place," Diane urged.

"I can't. You know I can't. I can't leave her here alone," Bernie had said.

There was so much about Bernie's relationship with her mother that Diane did not understand. Certain ways they interacted made her cringe but were, in the minds of the Chows, totally acceptable.

"We just don't waste time with politeness the way you do," Bernie had said.

But this was different. Bernie was being affected by her mother's abuse. It was awful. Week after week, Diane tried to get her to leave, but her pushes were turning into arguments. She was losing her connection with Bernie.

One evening, at the peak of one of their fights, Bernie told Diane to leave. "If you want to live somewhere else so much, just go and do it. Stop pushing me!"

Diane left.

Weeks later, Bernie called Diane, asking her to come by, saying she would leave with Diane.

When Diane arrived at the house, truck ready and waiting to take Bernie and her things, her mother was waiting.

"She not here," she said, watching Diane's face closely. "She don't want to live with you. She stay here."

Diane didn't believe her and started mounting a protest, but Bernie's mother cut her off. "You think I lie? Go to the restaurant, you see. She rather work than leave with you."

Diane drove by the restaurant and saw her. Working. Her mother was right. She had changed her mind.

೨

After Bernie's mother died, Diane called her again to see if anything had changed. She stayed for a few days, but in fact too much had changed. Sandy was a little boy. Bernie was more closed off than before. She had put herself through nursing school at a college a few towns over and was working at a hospital full time. She was never home. She didn't want her sister Jun to know that she was back together with Diane, so when Bernie learned that the sister and her little boy were planning to visit, Bernie asked Diane to stay away. Jun had left her husband a few years after moving down to the city. Something about an affair. Diane left one late summer evening, a couple days after she had arrived. She didn't leave a note. It didn't seem like it mattered anymore.

———·———

"HEY DIANE, YOU hear about Nelson?" She is walking up to the bar, a slab of wood thick with polyurethane, the grain visible but out of reach. Behind it, Dale, the owner, is working on a Friday afternoon.

"Nah, what happened? I didn't see him on my way in."

The light is falsely dim in Dale's Grill. The windows are mostly closed or covered with posters and neon signs. It is just bright enough to see the busily decorated walls, framed photographs, beer ads, baseball players. A Blue Jays 1992 team photo. Mirrors. Everything a particular story.

"He ain't here, Diane. He's passed away." Dale is standing with his arms at his side, not in their usual place resting on the bar or wiping it. "They found him this morning."

"Oh, hell. What happened?" Diane didn't know Nelson all that well, but they both ended up at Dale's in the late afternoon on a pretty regular basis. They spoke frequently, the idle meandering chatter of masculinity. All that Diane knew about him was that he had lived alone and worked most days helping out at a farm just out of town.

"Froze to death, out by the tracks," Dale says, breaking eye contact and resuming polishing the bar. "Beer?"

"Oh no. Yeah. Please." She sits down at the bar as Dale places a glass in front of her. Her hand wraps around the glass. She is lost for a moment as memories condense. Nelson was always keen to talk to her, which was nice. It helped the other guys in the bar warm up to her being the way she was. As in not interested in sex, at least with them. Nelson just talked to her like one of the guys. He seemed to pick her out of the crowd, not to hit on her, just to chat, to relate. The last time she had talked to him, Nelson had looked particularly exhausted. She had asked him how he was doing, and he had just looked at her long and quiet before saying, "Ah, *you* know." He had shaken his head and laughed, and said nothing more about it.

She didn't have a clue what he was talking about. She couldn't remember when that was. In the bar it was always the same in-between time of day, the same in-between time of year. Holding the beer in her hand, she turns to look out the window of the bar to see a young gay-looking kid tying up a dog on the steel pole outside. She watches for a second before realizing she's seen that dog before. It looks like Sandy's dog.

つ

Weeks later, after confirming a few more details, she decides to approach this young fey individual and make an introduction. Diane does not know it but senses that Mei's arrival is an opportunity for penance.

———

IT IS LATE spring. Mei has been alone for weeks, except for the occasional trip to town to get groceries or go to the thrift store. She hasn't found anything as nice as the velvet-lined case she found the first time. Her plant, sitting by the kitchen window, grows new leaves each week. They are thick, heart-shaped, and a brilliant green. When the phone rings, Mei doesn't expect it. Annette is away somewhere on the west coast, and Connie's phone has been disconnected again. Mei had tried calling her in the early spring. She had no reason not to have called more often, and she wishes she had. Mei picks up the phone—it is Diane.

"Hey you! You mind if I come over? I wanna talk to you about something." Diane is chipper.

If Mei knew her better she would say Diane's enthusiasm was forced. Her words are confident but terse. She had not expected to hear from Diane again.

"What do you want, Diane?" Mei hasn't interacted with anyone but Hazel in weeks, and she is happy to keep it that way.

"Hey, kid, I get it. I—I have something to say to you," Diane insists.

Mei doesn't know her well, but there is a tension in the words that makes her think that this is out of character.

"Say it now."

"I—the other week, when I came by for dinner, I said a couple things."

"Yes, Diane, you did say some things. What do you want?"

"I want—I want to apologize. Can I come over and talk to you in person?"

Mei relents. She is not sure why; perhaps she is ready to have company. Maybe she believes Diane. Both and neither could be true at once.

᷒

When Mei hears Diane's truck in the driveway she does not answer the door.

"It's open!" she calls out when Diane knocks.

Diane lets herself in. Mei waits in the kitchen. Diane is fidgeting, but present. She nervously says hello and asks mundane questions about Hazel, and she awkwardly gets a glass of water before sitting at the table.

"It smells in here ... Not in a bad way. It's familiar, like—" Diane inhales deeply, "like..."

"It's incense. I burn it every day. But you didn't come here to talk about how Sandy's house smells." Mei leans against the counter, arms crossed.

"I watched this documentary about this pipe fitter who used to be a man but then, when he was older and his kids had moved out, he tells his wife he's actually a woman. She can't deal with it at first, but then accepts him. It was really great. You should watch it."

Mei catches herself rolling her eyes, unimpressed. This had better not be why Diane came over. "Maybe that's something I don't need to watch as much as you do," Mei says shortly and stares at Diane, her mouth closed tightly.

"What's that supposed to mean? I don't have a problem with people like you. I just—"

"People like me? Half breeds? People with absent fathers? Or dead cousins? People with inherited dogs?" She is being unfair and she knows it. "Why did you want to come here, Diane?"

"The movie, it made me think is all. I don't know much about what it's like to be—"

"A transsexual? I'm listening."

"There's a lot I don't know. I was out of line."

Mei looks at Diane thoughtfully and decides the apology is sincere. She has not felt that about any such apology before. Usually, they are defensive precautions taken by people who are more afraid of looking like a bigot than being one. "Apology accepted."

Diane's face relaxes. She smiles.

"Why did you watch that movie, Diane?"

"My buddy, the one that passed away in the winter, Nelson. Nelson Hendricks. By the tracks, you remember me telling you about him?"

"Yeah. I remember."

"He said I should watch it. Said the lady in the movie was someone he'd met once through a job, years ago. That guy was full of surprises. I miss him, you know? We weren't close, but he was just always around when I was. Part of the routine." Diane's hands are on the table, holding each other. She looks at her knuckles, then leans back. "Anyway, that's not the point. The point is I watched it and it helped me see something."

Mei, silent, feels the muscles in her face relax as she steps forward and puts her hands in the back pockets of her pants.

"Do you want to say for dinner?" she asks. "I'm not sure what I'm going to eat, something though."

Diane pauses. Mei can't tell if Diane is surprised by the offer or considering it.

"Hey there, that plant!" Diane's focus shifts to the plant behind Mei on the counter. "That's Bernie's philodendron! I thought Sandy killed it." Diane smiles sadly.

"Yeah, it's doing pretty good right now. A philodendron. That's what it is?"

"Yeah. A heartleaf philodendron, I gave it to Bernie. I used to call it 'Phil.' You know, for short." Diane wrings her hands.

"Diane, are you gonna stay for dinner?" Mei asks again, smirking.

"Sure."

ɔ

Later, they eat dumplings Mei made weeks earlier and froze. Something Sandy had taught her. Mei expresses, as best as she can, why she does not want to watch the pipe-fitter documentary.

"I just think it's okay to want to know, that's all. Why shouldn't we hear her life story? It's interesting and it might change people's minds. And this way, people don't have to keep repeating themselves in person." Diane has apparently been pressuring all of her co-workers to watch the movie.

"But they do! Having stories like this just makes

people feel like they know me. Like they can ask me whatever they want." Mei is rearranging her bowl and chopsticks as she talks.

"But it makes it more relatable."

"Maybe for you! Not for me. It's like some people feel entitled to everything, the land we're on, who can stay, who has to go, what our lives are like. Why should I have to be relatable to get respect?" Mei is impassioned and mildly drunk.

A late spring night closes around them. Their eyes accept the dim kitchen light as the sun fades, making the room feel warmer than it had in the afternoon.

"I'm afraid about the example it sets. You remember when I first met you and asked if support was ever complicated for you?"

Diane leans back in her chair and laughs.

A boat drifts in the middle of the bay. Mei thinks about a neighbour she once had in the city. A gardener. The tenants who used the yard before the gardener had fixed their vehicles on the lawn, motor oil and chemicals soaking into the ground. She researched plants that could clean the soil, repair the damage enough to allow for growth. The plants would be poisoned, inedible, but after a few seasons, they would have cleaned up the ground. That was years ago. Mei wonders what vegetables she would be growing now. She wonders what happens to all the plants that grew up digesting the dirt. That depth of cleaning requires a sacrifice.

Last night, when Mei found herself in the front seat of Sandy's truck, she couldn't fall completely into sleep. She remembers the dream she had, almost completely, as she feels the gentle rocking of the water beneath the canoe.

A REUNION OF SAGES

MEI AND ANNETTE are standing outside of the community centre where their drop-in happens. It is cold, late November, a few months after Mei was attacked in the park. They are staring up at a flag that has been raised over the front door. Mei is drunk. It is the first time she has been to any kind of public event since that night in the park.

"I hate that flag. I've always hated that flag," she says, shaking her head.

"It's ugly. That's for sure," Annette agrees.

"More than that. It's offensive. It's gross! I mean *look* at it!" Mei's voice rises.

"Here we go..." Annette reaches into her purse and pulls out a cigarette. Lighting it, she exhales and leans back on one hip. "Okay, I'm ready. Make me really hate it."

Annette is not from this city. In the years they have been friends, she has never told Mei clearly where she is from. Mei knows she is from outside a city in another province, but she masterfully avoids speaking about it. As if it is omitted from her memory, a place she has forgotten how to return to. She does not share Mei's bitterness but loves this spark of life in her friend.

Ignoring Annette's sarcasm, Mei says, "Look at

it. Blue and pink. Blue and pink! Boys and girls. One, it's like the only thing that you can be is a boy or a girl, which is a totally white idea. Lots of other places in the past and right now have more than just boys and girls."

Annette's head turns, considering the colours.

Mei continues, "So that's stupid, but to really drive the point home, it literally, not even in some 'I'm not racist *but*...' undercover sneaky way, it literally is white in the middle. Talk about centring whiteness! Then they tell us it's the transgender flag and it represents us. It's the whitest thing around! At least the rainbow flag has sex and magic in it."

"Had sex and magic in it, honey. Had sex and magic," Annette corrects her. "And it's a *flag,* darling. A flag. What do flags do? They mark territory. And I don't let anyone piss on me for free."

Mei laughs loudly, validated. She looks up. "You hear? You should pay me to look at you!" Mei shouts at the flag.

"C'mon honey, let's take you home." Annette links arms with Mei and guides her to the bus.

———·———

WALKING WITH HAZEL through the woodlot, Mei finds herself in a conversation with Nai Nai. As if she is present, current.

"Why did you never move to the city with us?" Mei wants to know, the question hiding her real concern: was she not good enough to live with?

Nai Nai smiles, sucking her teeth. "When I was young girl, we live in the south. We did not live in the city. Each morning, I walk to the river for water. Some days I see cranes flying. You have never seen something so beautiful, Xiao Mei."

Mei cannot tell if she is imagining or hearing her grandmother's voice. She continues to wonder as she returns to the house.

᠑

"Darling, you sitting down?" It is Annette. Her voice is holding something back.

"Why? I prefer to stand while on the phone. I can pace, change rooms." Mei is standing at the kitchen table in Herbertsville, skimming through one of Sandy's journals, waiting for tea and looking out the window into the summer afternoon.

"Mei. I'm serious." Annette's voice has never sounded like this. Her usual confidence is absent.

"Okay. Okay. I'm sitting. What's up?"

"Connie's dead."

Mei lets the receiver drop from her face. Her hands stop idly flipping through the journal. She cannot hear what Annette is telling her.

"Mei?" Annette's voice is distant, separate from the moment she is living in. "Mei?"

"I'm here. What happened, Annette?" Mei says quietly, her voice raspy.

"She had some kind of heart attack or fever or something. She was really sick. But no one knew. She died at home. No one had seen her in a few days and someone called the super of her building to check in and they found her."

The kitchen walls have fallen away. A winter desert blows through the room. Hazel's fur shifts in the gusts.

"How long? How long has she been dead for?" Her voice is barely audible. The fragile pattern like Morse code on driftwood.

"Mei. I'm so sorry."

"How long, Annette?" She is nearly yelling now, her voice hot with desperation.

"...A month."

"No..."

"Mei. I just found out this morning. I called you right away. Right away. One of the staff at the drop-in called me. They didn't have a number for you. The staff said that she hadn't been coming to the drop-in for a while and they heard she had a cold."

"She was sick. I was here and she was dying." Mei's words fall out into the kitchen absently, their heat condensing on guilt, setting in, frigid.

"Mei. Baby. No one knew."

The July light shines through the back window, catching the philodendron. Its new growth cascading out of the pot.

"I tried calling her, Annette. I tried and her number wasn't working. I could have called you. I could have called the centre." Her mind is circling all the actions she didn't take.

"Mei. She left you some things."

Mei stops running through actions, retrieving mistakes, and listens to Annette.

"She left you a statue of a jade horse and a trunk. A huge trunk full of books."

Mei sits in the kitchen. Looking out into the desert she finds herself in, she makes a plan. She needs to get out of here. She needs to leave this house. She should have been in the city for Connie. For a death. For a funeral. Where was she buried? She should have found her. All the regrets of absence.

Annette has hung up the phone. Mei is still holding the line. Connie is dead. The words drown out the dial tone, then the regular beeping of the line, trying to get Mei to hang up. Connie is dead. She could have gone back to the city to visit. She has the truck. She could have called before the winter when Connie's line was disconnected. She could have taken care of Connie like Connie had taken care of her. Instead, she has been hiding in this empty library of a house. An obsessive record of memories. Dropping the phone on the floor, she stands and walks to the philodendron, which has recuperated. Healed. In one swift move she throws the plant on the floor, shattering the pot.

In Bernadette's room, Mei throws the suitcase with the velvet lining onto the floor and opens it. She opens the dresser and tosses some of her socks in the case. She needs to leave this place. She cannot stay in the house any longer. Everything she sees, everything she touches here reminds her of her absence. Her disrespect. She'll go back to the city. She can't go back to the city. What will she do there? She's abandoned her elder. Connie wouldn't have understood why she left. Mei never even told her about Sandy. Connie had no idea who Sandy was to Mei, that he was dead, or how his death had affected her. She just took off. Mei sits on the bed and looks out the window.

The goose is back, staring in at her. She had never told Sandy about Connie either. Two of the most important people in her life and she had not told them about each other. She needs a cup of tea. Or a shot of something. She gets up and walks into the kitchen. Ignoring the explosion of dirt and ceramic on the floor, she steps over the philodendron and puts the kettle on. She throws some food scraps in a bowl to offer to the goose.

ɔ

An hour later, sitting in the kitchen and looking out the back window, holding a half-empty cold cup of tea, Mei is startled by how dark it has become. She has been distractedly packing. Opening a drawer and walking away, leaving piles of clothes and snacks half sorted throughout the house. Rubbing her hands over her face, she decides to get up, to continue packing. Diane can watch Hazel. She doesn't need a destination.

Walking into Bernadette's room to get her things, she finds the dog surrounded by torn strips of red velvet, covered in lace, tail wagging. Garter belts, stockings, a bra, and beautiful lace panties she has never seen before are scattered across the floor. Mei realizes Hazel has ripped open the lining of the velvet-lined case. Looking at the mess, Mei suspects something was spilled in the case years ago that Hazel has picked up on. Whatever flash of anger she feels seeing the case destroyed fades with the revelation of its contents. She kneels down and looks more closely. She finds a faded envelope stuck under the last shreds of the lining. It is the size of a school notebook. It is heavy, and the paper has yellowed with age. Mei picks the envelope up and opens it, trying not to crack the paper. She finds a stack of photos of a group of drag queens. Mei catches herself; she has no reference for how these people saw themselves. The images are grainy, early colour photography. The people are posing—some as though they are at a pageant, some as though in a class portrait. Wearing beautiful gowns and costumes, they are standing in a drab, cigarette-stained hall. Each photo is set in the same place. It looks like a legion or a community centre. She can see a picture of a young Queen Elizabeth hanging on the wall in the background. Looking at the back of one of the pictures of a solitary broad-shouldered and proud woman, she reads a name.

"Aiya."

ↄ

The sun has broken the horizon and rises, sending red light through the front of the house. Mei has lit the last of Nai Nai's incense, and after paying her respects, leaves it burning in Sandy's room. She has been up all night packing her things, Sandy's things. She knows she doesn't need to take everything from the house, that she can come back whenever she wants, but she decides she needs to take some things with her. The ushanka, even though it is late summer. A picture of Nai Nai, Bernadette, and Jun. Snacks. She is only taking a backpack she found in the basement after Hazel destroyed the suitcase she had planned to use. Out of guilt, she has repotted the philodendron. It has a few broken stems but is otherwise unharmed. Locking the door with one of the three keys to the house, she leaves with Hazel and the plant.

As she is pulling out of the driveway in Sandy's truck with Hazel in the passenger seat, on her way over to Diane's, she sees the goose through the rearview mirror. It is standing just behind them. The bird waddles around to the driver's side, taking slow, purposeful steps until it stands a few feet away from the truck door. It turns its head to the side, and Mei could swear it is giving her a long hard stare.

"Weirdo winter goose. No wonder you weren't invited south with the others."

ɔ

"Thanks for watching her," Mei says to Diane, handing her a bag of Hazel's food. "I'll be back in a few days."

They are standing in Diane's driveway, a late summer morning breeze curling around them, carrying cool air and a promise of autumn.

"Where are you headed?" Diane asks.

"A friend's place, a bit north of here," Mei lies.

Diane nods, smiling. "I'm always happy to have the chance to help," she says, earnestly.

"Oh yeah, one more thing." Mei turns back to the truck. She reaches in and picks up the philodendron and the envelope of old photos of Herbertsville's trans women. She holds the envelope in her hand, having second thoughts about showing the pictures to Diane. They had been a secret for decades. Herbertsville is a small place; maybe it is better some things are kept secret. There was nothing to indicate that anyone wanted the pictures to be shown. She hesitates a moment longer and puts the photos back down on the passenger seat of the truck, taking only the plant.

"I thought you should have this. It's a tough little plant."

Diane's eyes redden as she gently nods.

Mei gets in the truck. Turning on the radio, Mei starts the truck and drives westward, to the lake. Diane waves to Mei awkwardly with a bag of dog food in one hand and the philodendron in the other, before walking back to her house with Hazel. Mei sees Diane look up to a flock of geese passing over. A solitary bird flies behind the flock, rejoining them.

The lake is an unstated truth. If you didn't know that it was coming, you'd have no idea you were on a peninsula. The flatness of the terrain doesn't show the drop-off to the lake. But after an hour, the treeline becomes a veneer. It becomes obvious that there aren't trees behind the trees you see, that the landscape changes just beyond what is visible.

The increased numbers of windmills may pro-
vide clean energy, but they are disrupting migratory bird
populations. Large numbers of birds have been found at
the base of the windmills, evidently struck by the blades.
That's not the only thing affecting birds in the area, Ted
Huntley reports.

Thanks, Jill. The recent expansion of a shoreline
golf course threatens the sensitive mating grounds used
by a bird that travels days to get there each year, the—

Mei changes the station, looking for a song,
something familiar.

At the lakeside, there is no place to park. The
lake belongs to the public but the access to it is private.
She drives north, looking for a place to pull over and
get to the water. The heat of the air above the water is
pulling up the lake and forming clouds with it. A storm
is building. It is late afternoon when she finally stops.

She sighs deeply and runs her fingers through
her hair. She cannot find a way down to the beach. All of
the land along the shore has been bought up by cottagers. She wants to pitch Sandy's tent, sleep on the sand,
watch the storm on the lake from inside its thin walls.
Veils of separation. She is not ready to feel a part of the
transfer of energy that is about to happen, the water in
the sky returning to the water covering the lake bottom.
Sandy would have just pitched the tent, a little out of
the way but not hidden. There is no place to hide on
the beach; the cottagers having made sure their views
are unobstructed. Any attempt to be concealed would
look suspicious to people who leave their screen doors
unlocked and their cottages unmonitored by security

systems. She thinks about trying to slip into a porch after dark and sleep there, but decides against it. If some county cop caught her in her little tent and dragged her out, what would they do? What do they do to vagrant transsexuals on the lake?

She gives up and walks back to Sandy's truck, which she has parked on a dead-end road nearby. Mei takes a deep breath. The isolation she felt in the city has shifted. Even though she is alone, it is somehow less painful to be alone and not see another person than to feel alone in a city. But she cannot stay in Herbertsville or in this truck forever. She hasn't heard Nai Nai's voice as clearly as she had before she left the city, but she is regularly talking to her, thinking with her. There was comfort in walking with silent company. She imagines she is walking with family, letting them see through her eyes. She watches the rain from the bench seat in the front. When the storm breaks, the windshield is submerged. She sleeps in a shell.

She dreams a conversation with Nai Nai. They are sitting on a large stone, out of place on a sandy beach. It is surrounded by evidence of other large stones that have been ground to dust by the weather around them, always aware of the next incarnation of their substance. It slowly wears away to merge with its grainy ancestors. A piece of the large stone has been broken off, by ice in the winter or a bored teenager. Nai Nai holds the piece of the rock, a piece too large to mix with the sand, but cut off from the bigger stone beneath them. She hands it to Mei.

"Take care of each other," she says.

When Mei wakes, it is still night, still raining gently. Sleepily, she imagines she had been drinking Connie's chrysanthemum tea. Connie had made it the last time they had seen each other.

"You have too much anger, Sai Mui."

The cold dry air of the coming autumn curled around Mei and Connie, who were walking through the park near Connie's apartment. Mei had just interred Sandy's ashes, something she had not told Connie.

"I am not surprised. How could I be? There are so many things to be angry with," Connie continued. She was older than Mei, by a decade. By two decades. Mei didn't know. She would never ask and would always be curious.

"I do not have too much anger. Whatever. What am I even angry about?"

"Your family. Not looking like you think you should. Too white." Connie looked at her young friend. "All around you are reasons to be angry. The people you meet. Someone looks at you the wrong way, someone says something at the wrong time, your paperwork gets turned down, the doctor treats you like a science experiment and won't give you hormones. Those are all great reasons to be angry. But it builds up, Sai Mui. It is all over you. I see you, holding anger like your child. Taking care of it. Quietly raising it."

Mei turned to stare at Connie, at this unexpected observation. There was no dirty joke to follow. She had not seen Connie this serious since she had been attacked in the park, nearly a year ago.

Mei met Connie at a drop-in, where Connie was handing out pieces of paper for an activity. The pages were a mix of colours. She handed the woman beside Mei a yellow piece of paper and said, "Yellow paper for the yellow lady," then handed Mei a white piece: "White paper for the white lady!" She then flashed the two unacquainted women a smile Mei would come to associate with Connie provoking trouble. She was testing Mei, who failed, incredibly. She did not return a cunning insult, but crumpled the paper in her hand, dropped it at Connie's feet, and walked out of the drop-in. Mei only returned months later with Annette, who used Mei's name loudly and complained about her own Chinese grandparents, saying they were too old to understand that not everyone wanted to sleep with people who looked like their own parents, making racial mixing bound to happen. Mei hadn't known Annette was going to pull something like that and was mortified. Blushing, she whispered for Annette to stop talking, but Annette had done what she set out to do. Connie made a sour face at the two of them. Annette, thinking she had done her part to make the space safe for Mei, never came back. She had other places to be, she said.

Mei didn't have other places to be, and kept going. It was another few months before Connie and Mei became friends. Mei, in a moment of bravery, had asked Connie some questions about growing up in Hong Kong and Connie, excited to be talking about something other than gender or hair removal, talked a lot.

That was years ago. Now they saw each other almost every week, and neither of them went to the drop-in.

"Too many conversations about surgery and if I am sexual or gendered," Connie had said, shaking her head and sucking her teeth.

Now, Mei was startled by her friend's use of metaphor. Her sudden concern for Mei's emotional well-being. "A baby of anger? What? Like a little green scaly horned lizard baby?" Mei laughed.

"Would you rather I said you were raising a little hard-on?" Connie grinned. Mei slapped her shoulder.

"You're the worst, Connie."

"Mei, the world is not going to stop being a hard place to live in." Connie's tone had become serious again.

"Obviously, Connie. What is up with you today?" Mei asked, gently touching her friend's wrist.

Connie smiled. "I was just thinking about you. I am cold. Let us go back to my place."

ɔ

The rain finishes. Starlight refracts through static water drops on glass. They are warped pieces of ancient light, catching her unable to sleep, kept up by memory. She is an unlicensed driver, illegally parked, protected by the absence of traffic, of street lamps. The truck had hardly been used all winter and spring. It is dusty and still has Sandy's work garbage in it. Coffee cups and sandwich paper are crumpled on the floor. There are broken pens on the dash above the radio, and a red and gold charm hangs off the rearview mirror. Diane had insisted that she at least start the truck once a week if she wasn't going to drive it or sell it. Mei would get in, start the truck, let it run, eyes focussed on the ignition, then straight out the window. She had no desire or ability to look at the rest of the truck and she didn't want to clean it. Every week she'd turned it on, dutifully. A reluctant ceremony of remembrance, an offering.

She wishes she could sleep. She is certainly tired enough. She has been looking at the photos of Herbertsville's trans women—if that's how they saw themselves. Beside her are two photos, one autographed with a heart and lipstick kiss: *To Nelson - all my love*. A photo of a beautiful young queen, *Nelson Hendricks, 1981* written on the back. The rest of the photos are safe in their envelope. She smells a cigarette. Turning away from the window, she looks up to see Sandy sitting in the passenger seat. Her eyes search for light to determine if he is real or not. Looking at him there, staring out the window calmly smoking and watching the night, his obvious comfort in the space is a grounding entitlement. Ghost or hallucination, she has missed him. She does not question his appearance for more than a second.

"Hey Mei. You're awake," he smiles at her. "Sorry I don't keep pillows here. There might be an old sweater or two behind the seat. Here, let me check." He reaches behind him. "Yup, here you go. I don't really need them." He drapes two sweaters over her. They are filthy, but warm.

"Thanks, buddy," she says sleepily. "What are you doing here?"

"I missed ya, and it looked like you needed a buddy." He puts the cigarette out in the ash tray. "Old habits..." He chuckles.

"Yeah. You're right. How is it being dead? It's gotta be weird."

Sandy laughs, tilting his head to one side, surveying her. "Right to the chase. Aiya. Well. I don't know. It *is* weird. I feel like I haven't really left. Like most of me is still here. Hanging out. I couldn't tell you what I get up to, but I just have that feeling, you know?"

She adjusts the sweaters and curls herself up on the seat. "No, Sandy. I have no idea."

"I suppose you wouldn't." He laughs softly.

She rests her head on the seat, smirking at him. When she opens her eyes next, Sandy is gone, but she has two sweaters on top of her. She turns the key in the ignition to get the dashboard lights on. The dull blue light of the digital clock comes on. The display is broken and tells her it is *h:_5* in the morning. She taps the display lightly to see if that will change the number: *t:h_*. She gives up and leans back in the seat.

"Xiao Mei." An old Chinese woman is knitting beside her in the truck.

Mei takes a deep breath, blinking. She does not recognize this woman. How has she gotten inside the truck? What is happening tonight?

The woman, not raising her eyes from what looks like a mitten says, "Why you sleep in this mess?" Her voice is familiar. It is Nai Nai.

Mei stares at her. Sandy's ghost was more approachable, more tangible. Nai Nai had died when she was much younger; maybe this is what she really looked like, but she is unfamiliar to Mei. Unsure of how to react, she decides to respond to the ghost.

"Nín hǎo Nai Nai. I'm sleeping here because all the cottagers bought the beach." Mei shrugs.

"You should get a nice job and buy one," Nai Nai says as she silently counts stitches, her lips moving as she does.

"Yeah. Yeah I should." Mei stares out into the night, focussing on the subtle differences in the shades of black and grey outside the truck. The night is not uniform.

"I want to tell you a story, Xiao Mei," she says. "You warm? I leave this in the box for you when they finish. I make them for Bernadette, but she doesn't want mittens so she give them to Sandy. He want gloves. No way to win. Now, a story.

"There is a forest, beautiful forest. The best forest. Many flowering trees and fruit. The trees all drop leaves, the leaves dry out and sit on each other. Time passes and there is mountain of leaves. Lots of leaves in the way. One day—"

A loud noise, a bang. Something hits the hood of the truck. An acorn or a pine cone. Mei looks quickly from side to side out of the windows of the truck, sleep thick in her eyes. She turns back to the passenger seat and Nai Nai is gone.

"Aiya," she mutters, closing her eyes again to fall asleep.

"Hey! Sai Mui!" says Connie. Connie is now in the truck. "You asleep? Because I don't blame you, the way your Nai Nai tells that story, I was falling asleep!"

"Connie?" Mei is confused. Ghosts of blood family somehow made sense, but Connie wasn't blood and besides, she had abandoned Connie. Maybe it was a punishment visit.

"Hello dear." Then, as if reading Mei's thoughts, "People are connected through more than blood, you know this. And, for the record, you didn't abandon me. You are still so angry."

Mei does not know how to incorporate what Connie is saying into her reality.

"You are cold, your Nai Nai left great mittens in the glove box." Connie opens it and pulls out two deep blue mittens. "So soft! She must have loved Sandy's mother!" Connie hands them to Mei.

"Not exactly," Mei says, putting the mittens on. "Woah, these *are* nice. Connie, what's going on? Why are you all showing up tonight?" Mei manages.

"That's not the question you should ask! It's pretty obvious," Connie grins. "I'm going to tell you a story. Your Aunt Bernadette told it to me. She said she tried to tell Sandy but he has too much to let go of before he can hear it. She's a really lovely woman, your aunt. Very interested in science radio programs. I like her. My son is also very into science. I wish I met Bernadette earlier. She could have helped me have a conversation with him." Connie pauses, reaches out to hold Mei's mittened hand. "Imagine a fire, Sai Mui. A forest fire. Those trees over there. On fire." Connie points out the window to the trees in front of the truck. "So in a forest, like the one we're in right now, fire starts when, this is how Bernadette said it, when 'conditions are made ripe for burning.' That's when the forest gets ready to burn. It takes very little for it to catch. It clears away all the stuff on the ground. Clears the way, leaves some carbon or something behind to help the trees in the future. But the fire needs something to burn to survive. Fire, it's almost a living thing, you know. That's why it's such a good killer. Which is useful in a dry old forest. Clear out the debris, make room. But that's only after the fire is out. You see, we need the fire to get rid of the circumstances that made it."

"What are you on about Connie? What are you, a secret botanist or something?" Mei is waking up.

"No, your aunt was, and she says your mother was too. Grew up in the woods in that town..." Connie looks thoughtfully at Mei.

"Herbertsville?"

"Yes! Herbertsville. But your mother isn't in a place I can talk to her. It sounds like she was a bit harsh with you." Connie puts a hand on Mei's arm.

"Yeah, she's not okay with transsexuals."

"Too bad."

"Connie, what happened? To you, I mean. I didn't even know you were sick."

Connie looks at her friend thoughtfully, eyes full of empathy. "I was sick for a long time, months at least. I kept on thinking I would get better, and I didn't want another social worker or well-meaning stranger to help me. At the end of the spring, I was still sick. I was always tired. You know, my son, he is a man, older than you, I haven't seen him since he was a boy. I'd been moving too much. And I decided to stop. It was time for me."

"But Connie, why didn't you call me, or anyone, I could have come back. I would have come back."

"Oh, I know Sai Mui, but I am happy with what is happening now. Besides, if I hadn't stopped fighting, I wouldn't have met your aunt and heard that great story. Isn't it a great story?"

Mei shakes her head, not wanting to accept what she is hearing.

"It got me thinking, Sai Mui. All the things that hurt you, all the things you are sensitive about, all scattered kindling all around your heart. And with enough pressure, enough heat, it burst into flames. That's the kind of anger you have."

"What's with you and telling me I'm angry?" Mei looks ahead, through the windshield, as she speaks, and she slides her hands around the steering wheel. "You want to know what I'm angry about? It's you telling me I'm so angry. It's you being dead, not letting me help you. It's—"

"It's important, Sai Mui. It's protection. That fire is a light. It lets you see everything that started this is as bad as it feels. You need the fire to see the kindling, to light the darkness, to burn away the nonsense." Connie pauses, looking out the window.

Mei can see her eyes following drops of water as they run down the windshield.

"So what's the problem with it? You're all—all warning me about it and stuff, but what you said makes it sound fine." Mei is frustrated by the heavy-handed metaphor.

Connie sucks her teeth and turns from the windshield to look at Mei. "That fire is going to help you see more and more things that make you angry, things that should make you angry. But if you've got that fire already raging away around your heart, and you keep letting those things feed that fire, you never get to have your heart back. It's too hot to touch. And the sound, have you heard the sound of a really big fire, Sai Mui?"

Mei does not answer, believing the question to be rhetorical, but Connie asks her again,

"Have you?" She does not want her lesson to be a lecture.

Mei is growing confused. "Yeah. Yeah, I have. Sandy and me used to make huge fires in his backyard. You couldn't stand too close to them, they were so hot. And they were loud. Really loud." She remembers the rumble and hiss of their bonfires. "We used to play this game where we would stand on either side of the fire and listen to the weird things it would do to our voices when we talked. Aunt Bernadette said it was something about the hot air affecting the sound of our voices."

"You see, Sai Mui? You have this fire and sometimes, if someone is trying their hardest to respect you, to tell you something you need to hear, you can't hear it because of the sound of the flames."

"So what, Connie? I hate getting advice."

"You hate getting help from people."

Mei doesn't respond.

"What if what they tell you gets warped by the flames? The way your and Sandy's voices would change over your backyard fires. All that anger, all the fire that sparked-off kindling, that's been piling for years, gets directed at them. Maybe they fit the shape of whatever started the fire to begin with. But they didn't start the fire. And you've been tending it." Connie's expression is stern and worried. "You need to deal with what started that fire. Then, those things that should make you angry, those people who challenge you, you can deal with them. With openness. With patience. With appropriate blasts of fire." Connie smiles, and Mei knows she added this to get a reaction from her. To lighten what she said. "You'll always find someone to help you stoke that fire, to help you direct all your rage away from the things you need to deal with to be able to keep your heart."

"What if I'm too far gone, Connie? What if—"

"You think we'd be wasting our time? Like I don't have somewhere better to be?" Connie shakes her head. "Aiya. Sai Mui, you'll always find someone to help make the fire bigger, but what we need is people who can help us control it. And that's not something I think you can do alone." Connie pulls Mei closer to her, out of the driver's seat, so she is leaning on Connie's shoulder.

Mei relaxes and leans into her. "Did you deal with it? Deal with your fire?" Mei asks.

"I'm dealing with it now."

The two of them stare out the windshield. Water pools along the still wipers and rolls off the truck.

"Connie, I'm so sorry I didn't know you better. Longer." Mei's eyes start to fill. Connie holds her tightly and says nothing as Mei starts to fall properly asleep. Nai Nai, sitting in the driver's seat now, gently strokes Mei's hair and sings quietly.

SANDY LOVES SUMMER storms, the chaotic balancing they bring. It is the end of August. A year since Mei was attacked. He puts his truck in park and pulls a cigarette out of his shirt pocket. Through the windshield he can clearly see the Herbertsville substation. The field is eerily level. At the right angle, it is impossible to see the shallow valley between where he is parked and the substation itself. Storm water drains through the valley and into the storm water management pond. The phrase makes him smirk: "water management." As if water can be controlled. Lighting his cigarette, he gets ready to watch the approaching storm. Grey-black clouds build on the horizon east of the station. He can still see the sun, clinging onto the day, as if pushed ahead by the storm. The dying light, thick like clean motor oil, holds as the rain breaks. Sandy exhales a cloud of light grey smoke and watches. This time last year he'd been wandering through the park where Mei was attacked, searching. He shakes his head, remembering the man he'd found that evening. The way he'd left him.

Watching the storm, Sandy sees something move inside the substation, catching the blue light of the small booth inside the fence. He watches the shape move, not erratic enough to be garbage. Wind pelts the truck with rain, making it hard to focus. The storm is in full force now. It is raining hard. Sandy feels like he is at sea in his truck. Through the rain-streaked windows he can barely make out the towers, faint masts on a massive deck. The wind pushes the grasses around in a careless rage, suddenly and erratically changing direction and speed. He has been training a new worker this week. She had lots of information about the job and was clearly good at school. It turned out she had been to university before going to college to be an electrician. She couldn't find work with her degree. He'd had a bit of trouble remembering all of the things he was never supposed to forget about the job—more to do with not being accustomed to having to articulate what he was doing than not doing it. At lunch on the first day he had taken her outside for a walk around the storm water management pond.

"Take away all the marshes, all the plants, pave over everything, and that water's gonna need to go somewhere. A big rain comes and if there's nowhere for the water to go, well, it'll find a place," she had said.

It made sense, he supposed.

"These ponds are funny to me, if we hadn't built a station where a swamp should be, or buried the streams that fed it, we wouldn't need to build an ugly square pond to flood. You said you planted it? It's full of invasive species. The whole thing looks out of place," she had said.

"We tried to plant native species but the geese just ate them."

She looked back at him with a sorry smile, the kind she might have given a friend for working extra hard to make dinner but forgetting the spices.

Now, watching the storm, he wonders about how the plants made it through storms like this. Which plants could hold the soil better and which roots had broken through the hard clay. He cannot make out what is moving inside the fence surrounding the substation. Leaning over the glove compartment, he digs for his binoculars. Lightning flashes. It's a goose. There's a goose wandering around the substation. Sandy exhales slowly, weighing options. He puts out his cigarette, throws on his raincoat and jumps from the truck into the storm.

Lightning is sparring the clouds, an erratic, brilliant dance that has a terrifying grace Sandy does not notice. At the fence, he picks up a few pieces of wet gravel and starts throwing them at the goose, who does not react.

"Get outta here! You crazy?"

The goose takes no notice, casually pacing around the gravelled area. He sees lightning advancing. Cursing, Sandy runs to the gate and steps into the perimeter of the substation, water streaming across his face. He yells to the goose, who turns to face him. A shudder strikes Sandy as he is overcome with the feeling that the goose has been expecting him.

ↄ

The sunrise hits the remaining clouds, soft red on grey-blue galvanized steel. The air is cold for August, cooled by the front brought in by last night's storm. The ground is still wet. A goose slides itself from under an arm where it has been protected from the storm. The gravel, though level, is uneven under its thin, webbed feet. It leaves before a maintenance crew arrives to fix the damage from the storm. They are one worker short, unable to reach him. There is no one to speak for his absence. Surprised to find his truck parked at the substation, they find him, unmoving and face down on the ground of the substation, cold in the quickly warming daylight.

M EI GETS A phone call while she is at home. The summer has stretched the days and widened the light. There is a visibility, a clarity to summer light that Mei is uncomfortable with. Too much definition, too clear a picture. It offers none of the forgiveness of narrow fall and winter light. It is late morning in Dundurn. Through the front window in her apartment, she can see the sidewalk outside is still wet from last night's rain, litter and leaves stuck to the pavement. Answering the phone, she hears a man she has never heard before and will never hear again. This momentary stranger brings information that changes every following moment. The man tells her that Sandy's body was found early this morning. He was electrocuted at a transformer station during the storm last night. He says it was probably a "lightning-triggered flashover." Why was he in a transformer station during a storm? The man on the phone doesn't know. It wasn't for work. There's a lawyer that will call with details. Mei is the next of kin. The man on the phone is very sorry.

Mei stands, her mind a block of wood, staring at the pavement through the window as the sun evaporates what is left of the rain.

—————

S HE WALKS AS close as she can get to the shore from the main roads. It is almost evening again, and she does not want to sleep in the truck another night, curled up in a ball. Her back aches. Besides, she needs to get out into the bay. There is a paved trail, a remnant of the railroad lines crisscrossing the country. Sandy would have something snide to say about the path, torn up so cottagers could walk their dogs and bike around after the rail lines had been starved out by highways and transport trailers. He hated and loved the railroad simultaneously. Or maybe he hated the railroad, but he hated highways more. It doesn't matter now. The bike path runs behind cottages that face the lake. After a few cottages with all their lights out and no cars in the driveway, Mei finds a summer camp. What is she doing? This is rash, unplanned and probably reckless. She had just filled a backpack and taken Sandy's truck. She's parked the truck at the head of the paved rail path. Now, twenty minutes later, she finds a path to the water. The moon is young, faintly lighting the beach.

"Finally," she whispers. She comes to a boathouse and small beached dock. The moon pours grey-blue light over the weathered boards. Someone has left a pair of goggles. There is a rack of canoes and a fire-pit. She looks around. She is on a small bay which she decides has to be pretty shallow. Wetland plants are growing up out of the water, and she can see bulrushes and reeds along the shore. The landscape oscillates between lake and marsh. She walks to the firepit and sits on a small bench. She kicks at the dead coals in the pit. Sandy had taught her how to light a fire when she was visiting one summer. Looking around the beach she sees a small pile of wood. The logs on the top layer are still damp from the rain the night before, but the third layer is mostly dry. She picks a couple of logs and takes them back to the firepit. A few minutes later she is starting a fire with newspaper she threw in the backpack before leaving Sandy's house and kindling she's pulled out from under the beached dock. Soon, she is sitting facing the bay, listening to the soft lapping of the water and warming herself with the fire.

She is mesmerized by the fire, holding a stick and poking at the coals. She puts down the stick and tosses in a couple of small twigs. They crackle and burn. *You've been tending it.* She remembers Connie's warnings. *You never get to have your heart back.* She gets up and kicks apart the logs, spreading the fire out. She tosses beach sand on the hot coals. The lake, a constant witness, says nothing.

She wants to get off the land. Approaching the rack of canoes, she sees they are chained up and locked with a small padlock. Through the window of the boathouse, she sees a wall of lifejackets and paddles. Everything you'd need to take fifty kids out into the water. The boathouse is locked as well, with the same small padlock. Sandy left tools in his truck. It is the middle of the week, and there aren't any cottagers around. She walks back to the truck.

It is easy to cut through the locks. She isn't going to take anything permanently, just borrow it. Maybe. Or maybe she will just keep paddling.

In the boathouse she sees names and numbers all over the walls. Brittany had been there in '99. Dave in '05. Names and years, written with the assumption that the record would persist and someone would want to read it. The building is small, one room and two small changerooms within it. It is packed with pool noodles and life jackets and paddles and first aid supplies. The names are a record, a warning and a challenge. This place is loved. Mei isn't going to trash anything, but she needs a paddle. After examining several, she picks one and heads out the door, stopping in the doorway to take a life jacket.

"I can sit on it," she says to herself.

She picks the canoe on the bottom, a yellow fibreglass one. There is a chain wrapped through all the canoes. Mei takes Sandy's large bolt cutters and splits the lock. As she threads the chain through the rungs of the canoe, the sound of the links banging the aluminum rungs grinds against the quiet lapping of the bay, cracking open the silence. The boat is light and easy for her to launch. She feels the shift in gravity from standing to floating, feeling as if her weight has changed. Submerging the paddle, she pushes herself out into the middle of the bay.

ɔ

She is in a stolen canoe. No one should know how to find her, but somehow Sandy is there with her. After his appearance in the truck yesterday night, his sudden arrival tonight is less shocking.

"You know what, Mei, I'm sorry I didn't tell you about Ma. It would have been really great if you two had got to know each other, you know, the way you really are," he confesses.

"Sandy, don't worry about it. I got to know Diane. She thinks you're great, you know?" Mei reaches over, gently rocking the boat, touching his shoulder. "Besides, Aunt Bernadette must have had a good reason not to want you to tell."

"She was afraid, Mei. I don't know of what. Something she never told me. Be careful with Diane. She's, well, she's not always reliable." He leans closer to her in the blue-black night. "But you know what? I forgive her for being such a crap support to my mother. And me, I suppose. It's easier, mind you, now that things have changed." Sandy smiles, sadly. "It's like a stone, anger. A grudge. You're supposed to use it to break through something. Then let it go. Like a, like a—"

"A thunderstorm?" Mei offers.

"Yeah, just like that. I was looking for a more poetic kinda word," he shrugs.

"Being dead sure made you sensitive," Mei teases. "Also, I thought you hated boats."

"Oh I do, there just aren't the same consequences anymore, I'm sorry to say. I would love to hate this boat right now, but I can't." He shakes his head, dipping his hand in the water. The water does not ripple.

"Hey Sandy, is heaven really just another

bureaucracy? You know, like with the Jade Emperor and stuff?"

"Ha! I wouldn't know ... Anyways, I forgive Diane; she and I don't have the kind of connection you and I do, so I can't really tell her. But I paid her a visit not too long ago. When I saw her at your place I wanted to bite her face off. But after that I went by her place—she is a lonely, lonely woman. I saw her sitting on her stairs in the morning, waiting for the time to leave for work. It didn't make me feel better about her or what she'd done, but it just—it just made her make sense."

Mei listens, staring out into the lake.

"Seeing her like that, understanding it, it felt like I'd thrown a huge stone out of my pocket. An impossibly cold, black, heavy stone."

"Sandy, I can't stand myself right now."

"I know. Go back to the city. Go see Annette. You think she doesn't need someone now too? So you weren't there for Connie—" he starts to say.

"It is a huge deal that I wasn't there for Connie! She took care of me. You wouldn't get it. How amazing it is to meet someone like you who's older, when you've been living with the idea that no one like you ever *gets* to be older. How incredible and terrifying it is. All at once." Mei is looking in his eyes, her own welling with tears. "I disappeared for almost a whole year. Went through your stuff. Lived in your empty house. And now Connie..." She is starting to cry for the first time in longer than she can remember.

"You need to forgive yourself," Sandy says, leaning back.

"What? For what Sandy? You're still so—so paternal!" She is crying fully now, her words refracting through tears.

"Mei..." Sandy says softly, "You know what I'm getting at. You know. Look at you. Out in a lake, in your city girl idea of the north. Like you're Frankenstein or something."

Mei looks up, confused. "What do you mean?"

"You know, Mei. You already know." He reaches out, his hand gently tightening around hers. Then he is gone into the night surrounding her.

ॐ

Water. Water surrounds her. Through her tears, the night changes shape. Dim moonlight and faint stars give contrast to the world around her. The sound of the lake on the shore, gentle footsteps. Her Nai Nai practicing taiji in the backyard, as the sun rose. The constantly shifting meeting point of water and sand, the careful placement of each movement. Nai Nai had tried to teach her when she was small, too small to remember. After her death, neither she nor Sandy could remember the slow dance she would perform alone each morning. Movements with mythic names. Wave Hands Like Clouds. Carry Tiger To Mountain. Each step shifts into the next. Tigers become geese, retreat from monkeys, and bury needles on the sea floor. Mei looks to the shoreline blurred by the growing lake in her eyes and sees each movement that brought her here, to the bay. She sees herself being attacked, Herbertsville, Diane. She sees her family moving like endless branching limbs spreading, moving away from each other, colliding with other moments, other branches. She sees Nai Nai, leaving China with Ye Ye, Mei's grandfather. She sees his death soon after arriving in Canada. Bernadette and Jun, small children alone with their mother in a strange land. She sees all this moving toward her at tremendous speed. At the moment of impact they engulf her and branch out in all directions, scattering across the surface of the lake. She is a moment on a spontaneous trajectory, her ancestors and descendants surrounding her, like water. Connected by blood and intention.

She reaches into her pocket and brings out a cell phone. Turning it on, she waits for it to wake. There is reception in the middle of the bay. She dials a number.

"Hey. It's me. Where am I? Oh, nowhere special. I was thinking of coming back in a couple of days. Can I stay with you? Maybe you'd want to come back here with me? What's what sound? Oh that. It's a lake. Yeah I'm in a canoe. No, I don't have one. I stole it. No, it is not pink. That joke is not only dirty and gross, but also not funny. Whatever, Annette. Love you, too."

ABOUT THE AUTHOR

jia qing wilson-yang is a mixed race trans woman living in Toronto. She likes to write poems and stories and music. Her writing has appeared in *Bound to Struggle: Where Kink and Radical Politics Meet* (ed. Simon Strikeback), *Letters Lived: Radical Reflections, Revolutionary Paths* (ed. Sheila Sampath), and the women of colour issue of *Room* magazine. She has recorded several acoustic albums and this one time was a drummer in a pop punk band. *Small Beauty* is her first novel.

ABOUT THE PUBLISHER

Metonymy is a Montreal-based press that publishes literary fiction and nonfiction by emerging writers. We try to reduce barriers to publishing for authors whose perspectives are underrepresented in order to produce quality materials relevant to queer, feminist, and social justice communities. We really want to keep gay book lovers satisfied.